"I never intended to fool you for long."

"Oh, what a lie!" Athena whispered scornfully. "When I think of how shabbily you've twice behaved, it puts me quite out of patience."

"But surely you don't mean to have a turnup with me here at your aunt's concert," Giles murmured. "Consider what a spectacle we should make."

She gasped, stung into an unladylike desire to spin around and box his ears. "To think that you should lecture me about appearances—when all the time it is you who has been suspect in your conduct!"

"Doubtless," he agreed readily, much to her confusion. "Though how inelegant of you to say so."

Athena was silent. If only he'd acknowledged that his actions had misled and humiliated her . . .

THE GRAND STYLE
LESLIE REID

Harlequin Books

TORONTO • NEW YORK • LONDON
AMSTERDAM • PARIS • SYDNEY • HAMBURG
STOCKHOLM • ATHENS • TOKYO • MILAN

In remembrance of
Augusta (''Tommy'') Atkins, 1902–1958,
who taught me the distinction
between knowledge and learning.

The Grand Style: A style of painting
suited to the expression of noble themes
and heroic subjects on a grand scale.

Published September 1986
ISBN 0-373-31014-5

CHAPTER ONE

ONE LOOK ABOUT THE ROOM she'd just entered had little effect on the frown that ruffled Athena Lindsay's brow. True, she sometimes took pleasure in the country scene exposed by the new French windows— a costly innovation but assuredly, in 1818, already the height of fashion in London. But the late-April light also revealed a threadbare Turkish carpet and a mended sofa among the paintings and rolls of canvas that overflowed every surface.

Athena threaded her way across the room, removed a painting from beneath one of the piles and propped it on an easel. First throwing a woolen smock over her gown of black merino and stirring the fire that fought bravely against the room's ever-present chill, she stood back and gave the painting a brief examination. With a sigh she selected a tube from the paints laid out on a table by the easel and daubed a bit of color onto a palette. Then she picked up a camel's-hair brush and began to work on a section of the canvas in a shade known as Egyptian brown.

It was approximately an hour later that the door of the studio was quietly opened by a perennial, if legitimate, visitor. Thus was Mr. Horace Pennington granted a private view of his mentor's only daughter—and the object of his romantic attentions.

Miss Lindsay's attire had as usual, Mr. Pennington noted disapprovingly, been selected with an eye to practicality rather than style. Every item was clearly serviceable and just as clearly lacking the signature of true fashion. Yet even these poor garments failed to conceal an elegant figure, or dull the effect of the expressive green eyes that elevated their owner's countenance above ordinary prettiness. His expression softened at the sight of a tangle of dusky curls, a straight and shapely nose and a pair of high-arching cheekbones set in a delicate, heart-shaped face.

It was while Mr. Pennington was considering how to advertise his presence that the focus of his observations became aware of him.

"At last, the valued protégé," Athena exclaimed smoothly. She offered a rare and therefore distracting smile as she lowered a drape over her canvas. "But pray enlighten me, sir. Can it be that you've come to wield a brush—or merely to play the gapeseed?" She fixed her visitor with a politely interested look.

"My dear Miss Lindsay, whatever can you be about?" Mr. Pennington bleated, flustered at having had the initiative plucked from his grasp. Wearing a solemn but solicitous expression, he advanced toward Athena, fluttering his hands earnestly as he spoke. "Such a delicate situation! You have my every sympathy! A tragic loss! But one wonders if you should be working so soon after—? Not," he corrected himself hastily as Athena's gaze turned arctic, "that I attribute your presence here to any want of feeling! However, I venture to say there are some people who might be provoked by such a failure to observe the proprieties!''

"And was it with a view to the proprieties that you decided to risk censure yourself in order to inform me of my duty—though it lacks scarcely twenty-four hours since poor papa was nailed up?'' Athena inquired curiously. She stopped, struck by a sudden dreadful thought. "Is this how you imagine it will now be, then? You will continue to visit prospective clients, as Papa did, in order to convince them of the many benefits and high quality of our portraiture, whereas I shall carry on with the more mundane task of seeing to the completion of the work?''

"There you have it!'' Mr. Pennington exclaimed smiling triumphantly. "After all, it would be most improper if a lady were to concern herself with shillings and pounds.''

"To be sure, I hadn't entirely considered how we were to manage,'' Athena admitted, pausing to study her companion as she cleaned her hands on an old cambric rag.

Mr. Pennington was dressed as usual in what he believed to be the proper attire for a fledgling man-about-town. However, his breeches, chosen to display a well-formed leg, instead revealed a pair of spindly calves, and his coat encased shoulders that would never have been called broad. His mousy hair was cropped and disheveled in imitation of a fashion plate from a recent issue of Ackermann's *Repository of Arts.* But in the end all his efforts only served to highlight a countenance dominated by a pair of protuberant and nearly colorless eyes, a receding chin and a sheen of perspiration along a thin upper lip.

"Can it be, sir," she inquired abruptly, "that Papa appointed you my representative?"

"Well, no, not precisely," Mr. Pennington admitted. "But I fancy you haven't been insensitive to my devotion to your honored father. Why, that a painter of his stature should have allowed me to assist him in my small way has been beyond anything great!"

Athena gazed down at him from the vantage point of an additional four inches in height. She'd often heard more objective critics dismiss Roderick Lindsay as an adequate, if unoriginal, painter. And certainly her own experience had revealed her father's artistic talent to be taxed by even the simplest portrait.

Promptly mistaking her silence for confirmation of his sentiments, Mr. Pennington crept a few steps closer and continued more boldly. "To be truthful, I must confess it's long been my secret hope that someday you might look on me as so much more than your father's assistant. Indeed, I flatter myself that if he hadn't been struck down in so untimely a manner he wouldn't have been entirely loath to entertain my suit." He smiled modestly, and having moved within range, tried to claim possession of Athena's hands.

"Your suit?" she exclaimed incredulously, pulling herself away from his grasp. "You can't honestly believe that we'd make a good match."

"My dear Miss Lindsay," Mr. Pennington puffed, doggedly pursuing the hand she'd thrust behind her, "what could be more suitable than that Mr. Lindsay's assistant and Mr. Lindsay's daughter should find their affections to be engaged? After all, I've frequently expressed to you my appreciation of your many excellent qualities."

"Quite," Athena agreed dryly. "Do I take it then that you don't suppose others might find our appearance together a trifle odd?" She stared pointedly down into his upturned face.

"Oh, pooh! What care do we artists have for convention?" he proclaimed.

"And no doubt you've also heard that my disgraceful tongue and my unfortunate habit of speaking my mind will be my ruination," Athena persisted. "I should think you'd find it endlessly inconvenient to be bound to a woman so disinclined to be biddable."

"To be truthful," Mr. Pennington responded manfully, "I long ago concluded that this darker side of your nature developed because of the lack of affection shown you by your family—your late father, though well-intentioned, being forced to concentrate on the business at hand and your dear mother being reluctant to attend to anything not writ down in some book."

Although Athena was inclined to agree with him, she refused to give ground before the puff toad who now smirked up at her. "I beg you not to tease yourself about what I can only term my personal affairs, sir," she added coldly. "Besides, it's common knowledge that I'm not possessed of any fortune, and you, too, are hardly plump in the pocket. How is it that you propose we might set up housekeeping?'' She offered him a bland smile.

"But can't we continue just as we are?'' he asked in confusion, dabbing at his upper lip with a lace handkerchief kept ready for that purpose. "My own skill isn't remarkable, it's true, but with your father's reputation to recommend us and your excellent assistance, I believe we'd acquit ourselves well enough.''

Athena couldn't suppress a burst of laughter. "Oh, famous!'' she exclaimed. "Hardly rid of one set of shackles before another set presents itself to view! It appears that I'll never be allowed to put my own wishes first. Rather, I should resign myself to catering first to one bobbing block and then to another. Well, I won't be relegated again to a mere shadow existence. And what's more,'' she added, turning to glare at Mr. Pennington, "if you truly imagine that your proposal will change either my resolve or my temper, then you're a bigger widgeon than I thought. Allow me to remind you, sir, that I didn't cut my wisdoms yesterday. I fancy you thought this the perfect time to find out whether you couldn't capture the golden egg and the goose, as well.'' She took a step forward, forcing Mr. Pennington to begin a retreat. "Well, sir, let me advise you that your scheme won't fadge. I am, of course, much obliged to you for making me an offer. However, I fear I must decline. We would not, you must certainly agree, deal at all well together.''

Trapped now between the door of the studio and Athena's formidable countenance, Mr. Pennington, to his credit, made one last attempt. "But what," he asked piteously, "shall you do?"

"That won't be of the least concern to you," Athena declared bluntly, propelling him out of the room and shutting the door in his face.

"SO YOU SEE, MAMA," Athena concluded a half hour later, "if I hadn't been so incensed, I'd have gone into whoops at the very prospect of being linked to that mushroom." She jumped up from the sofa to tug irritably at the drape on her painting before casting herself down again with a resentful thud. "No doubt he thought I'd prove endlessly grateful to have finally snared a husband at the antiquated age of eight-and-twenty. Far more likely, though, that my father's assistant seeks to imitate him in life as well as in art, since he might reasonably expect that my prospects, slight as they are, will serve to secure his future, just as you—"

She broke off at the stricken look on her mother's face, shifting uncomfortably in her corner of the sofa. "Oh, pray forgive me, Mama. Whenever will I learn to curb my wretched tongue?"

"Never mind, love," Mrs. Lindsay murmured as one hand twisted the gold band circling a dimpled finger. "How could I suppose that you'd understand?" She hesitated before confessing awkwardly, "At the outset, you see, I didn't dream that my marriage might turn out to be one of convenience. I was so terribly young...and I thought—''

''Please don't, Mama,'' Athena pleaded, patting her arm consolingly, as she had ever since she was a child. ''To be sure, this is an altogether different story. Besides, I'd think myself moonstruck if I ever agreed to tie the knot with such a dead bore. So don't tease yourself any further on that head.'' *And more to the point,* she added to herself, *I haven't the slightest wish to be married to Mr. Pennington or to any other gentleman.*

She paused to consider how to introduce the subject that dominated her thoughts. Finally, she asked in a tentative voice, ''Mama, are we aground?''

''Pray, what—?''

''What I mean to say is will our creditors soon be swarming round to collect their due?''

Mrs. Lindsay gave a start. ''Why, I'm sure I couldn't say!'' she exclaimed, looking horrified at the idea. ''Roderick, you see, always used to deal with— oh!''

''Quite so. Now, then,'' Athena continued patiently, ''do you perhaps recall, ma'am, what amount your godmama may have settled on you?''

Screwing her face up in an attempt to concentrate, Mrs. Lindsay at last offered, ''I'm not entirely certain, but I believe it may be a hundred pounds or so a year.'' She peered anxiously at her daughter. ''Will that serve, do you think?''

Athena shook her head reluctantly. ''No, I think not. Oh, we'll have sufficient to go along well enough for the time being, since neither of us is used to indulging in fripperies. So don't fall into a fit of the dismals. I'm sure I can think of a way for us to realize the necessary funds." She gave her mother's arm another encouraging pat.

A brief silence ensued during which Mrs. Lindsay alternated between wringing her hands in a ladylike fashion and staring hopefully into her daughter's face.

"It appears to me that we have two choices," Athena said slowly. "First, we may indeed continue just as we are, since Mr. Pennington assures me he'd be most willing to assume the responsibility of managing the studio. Though I confess I shouldn't like it overmuch and I fear I'd soon find his everlasting smugness beyond enduring." She plucked at a spot of paint on her smock as if to pluck up her courage. "Now our second course might prove a trifle more difficult at the outset. What I propose, you see, is that I apply my talents with a brush to securing employment as a painting instructress."

"Oh!" Mrs. Lindsay exclaimed unhelpfully.

"Of course, I know my skills aren't truly extraordinary," Athena hurried on. "Still, I believe my mastery of watercolors is quite creditable, and that, after all, is what most parents wish their daughters to learn."

"Oh!" Mrs. Lindsay said again. "But where should you find your pupils?"

Yes, where? Athena wondered.

"Didn't you tell me, ma'am," she inquired suddenly, "that you've received a letter from my father's sister? And didn't you also say that she invites us to stay with her for a time until we recover from our loss?''

"Yes, but—"

"Then that's the ticket, Mama! We shall go to London!" she exclaimed. "I can't think why I didn't conceive of it sooner. Aunt Louisa's been on the town for simply ages and must count everyone of the first consequence as her acquaintance. If she'd be so obliging as to introduce us here and there, I daresay I should easily be able to discover a sufficient number of her friends whose daughters—as I shall convince them—are sadly in need of instruction in the arts.''

Mrs. Lindsay began to chew on her lower lip, a sure sign that she was seriously discomfited.

"What's amiss, Mama? Shouldn't you like to go to London?" Athena asked, gazing wistfully around the narrow confines of her father's studio.

"Oh, no— That is, yes. I mean, it's only that I truly couldn't feel comfortable about taking advantage of Louisa's hospitality in such a hoaxing manner. And what's more, I'm positive she wouldn't like it a jot. Your aunt has always had the strictest ideas about what's becoming for a lady of quality, and this plan most assuredly is not.''

"Then we won't tell her," Athena said promptly. "Come, Mama," she coaxed, "let's not brangle about it. I don't mean that we'll tell her a lie, precisely, merely that we'll wrap it up in a little clean linen. Perhaps if you'd agree to look on this scheme as a sort of adventure— After all, one might almost say we're setting out to seek our fortune.''

"Oh!" Mrs. Lindsay cried enthusiastically. "Why, so we are, love. Just like Miss Austen's heroine in—''

A knock at the door, followed by the entrance of their elderly maid, served to interrupt one of Mrs. Lindsay's favorite literary tales.

"Mr. and Mrs. Dillingham, ma'am, to pay their respects," Doris intoned in the solemn voice she thought fitting to the occasion.

"Now, you may safely leave everything to me," Athena promised as she steered her mother's plump, diminutive figure toward the door. "I'll join you after I've composed a suitable note to my aunt."

Locating pen and paper, she cleared a worktable of paints and pulled it over to the sofa. Then she took up the pen, dipped it into the inkwell and proceeded to chew on the nib for several minutes. However, it wasn't the letter to her aunt that prompted this behavior but her need to examine the beginnings of another idea she'd wisely decided not to confide to her mama.

Now, it was true that whenever her father had been between commissions, she'd been able to snatch some time to sketch her own designs, and a fat wad of drawings now lay in the back of her wardrobe. Still, these exercises had left her dissatisfied, because she knew no one willing and able to supply an honest appraisal of her work. Her father, she had been sure, aware that his daughter's skill easily rivaled and perhaps outdistanced his own, was not inclined to help her. But if, Athena reasoned, she and her mother were to go to London to locate pupils, couldn't she at the same time seek the very criticism—and even the instruction—she so dearly desired?

However, if her aunt might cast a rub in the way of the first scheme, her mother, she imagined, would certainly protest once she learned that her daughter intended to set up as a serious painter. And given that circumstance, surely she had no choice but to keep her second purpose from both of them. So play a deep game she would, she decided at last, and no one need be the wiser.

Then, much cheered by that resolve, she dipped her pen into the inkwell again and began to write.

THE FEELINGS OF the two occupants of the hired post chaise rattling through London a week later were not altogether those of two adventurers seeking their fortune. Indeed, Mrs. Lindsay, huddled in her corner, prayed aloud for a speedy arrival only to ease her brutal headache, induced by the jolting. As for Athena, however, from the moment they'd entered the outskirts of the city, she'd been unable to drag herself from the window, so fearful was she of missing some wondrous sight.

Lamplighters mounting their ladders to kindle the gas orbs helped illuminate a scene in which confusion appeared to reign supreme. But it was the faces of the people they passed that mainly claimed Athena's attention. Street vendors hawked everything from hot pies to gaudy broadsheets. At the mouth of an alley a soldier lounged on crutches beside a tavern called Strip-Me-Naked. And once, when the chaise halted so that a maroon-and-black mail coach could thunder past, a girl of about thirteen with a baby at her breast approached the carriage window and stared in at the Lindsays.

Stunned by the impact of these scenes, both travelers expressed a sigh of relief as the coach drew up at last before one of a row of impressive houses in Grosvenor Square.

"Her ladyship asks if you'd be so kind as to await her in the drawing room," the butler said, showing them into a salon made comfortable with elegant furniture and damask draperies. "She's to join you directly. At the moment, I understand, she's in conference with Cook," he concluded darkly.

Mrs. Lindsay dropped into an armchair, holding out her hands to the fire that burned invitingly in the grate. Athena was just about to follow her mother's example when the door opened to admit Lady Hollinwood.

"My loves! Too bad of me not to greet you, but that stupid woman would argue that a cream sauce was nicer with sturgeon than the truffles I'd ordered. As if I wasn't aware that truffles are frightfully expensive—" Her ladyship broke off, recollecting her duties as hostess. "No, don't get up, Meg," she continued, advancing to plant a kiss on Margaret Lindsay's brow. "Why, you must be simply fagged to death. I daresay I would be. Shall I ring for some refreshment?" she asked hopefully. Upon being assured that her sister-in-law desired nothing more than to seek her bed, Lady Hollinwood pulled a bell cord. Then, turning toward her niece, she offered a scented cheek and exclaimed, "Come give me a kiss, child. I declare I haven't seen you this age."

Athena, who'd been gazing awestruck at her modishly attired relative, hastened to comply. Then she stood quietly, making an effort to appear composed under a frank examination that took in her old-fashioned bonnet, her dowdy pelisse and the soiled gloves she now thought to stuff into her reticule.

"Well, I see I may call you child no longer," Lady Hollinwood declared archly, smiling with obvious approval at the slender figure before her. "Scorsby will show you to your room directly, my love," she told Mrs. Lindsay. "And perhaps you, at least, will join me for a little supper," she said to Athena in a tone that required no answer.

MOST OF THAT GENEROUS MEAL took place in the silence that Athena decided her aunt felt appropriate to the serious business of obtaining sustenance. And although she was able to force down only a little soup and a few bites of the controversial sturgeon, Lady Hollinwood dealt in turn with a goose-and-turkey pie and a fricassee of chicken, a generous helping of orange soufflé and four meringues.

"Come to town to catch a husband, have you?" Lady Hollinwood asked suddenly with a knowing smile. "You needn't think I wouldn't find out, child. Well, I mean—what other reason could you have?"

Instantly perceiving the wisdom of encouraging her aunt along those lines, Athena at once exclaimed in an admiring tone, "Precisely so. I was sure we wouldn't succeed in humbugging you, ma'am. The fact is," she confided, "I've rather dished myself up at home. My father's assistant, you see, has grown uncomfortably particular in his attentions and has sought to fix his interest with me. So Mama and I determined to accept your invitation in the hope that we might thereby discover a more suitable match."

"And high time, too, I must say!" her ladyship exclaimed indignantly. She wiped her mouth and laid her napkin beside her empty plate. "Can't think what Meg was about, allowing Roderick to keep you both hidden away all these years. But then he always was bacon brained." Fixing her niece with a defiant look, she said, "I daresay you think me an unfeeling thing to speak that way about my own brother."

"Why, to be sure, I hadn't considered, ma'am," Athena replied innocently, greatly entertained by her aunt's speech. "And at any rate, your experience of him was much longer than mine."

Lady Hollinwood gave an appreciative laugh. "So you've a quick tongue. Far better to my mind than being a mealymouthed female. Still, there's no getting around the fact that you ain't an heiress, so you'd best learn to curb that habit of speech if you mean to get on." Her eyes narrowed a trifle as she examined Athena thoughtfully. "Not but what your looks ain't half bad. We'll just trim them up with some new clothes."

"But Mama and I are in mourning, ma'am," Athena pointed out. "Surely it wouldn't be right to—"

"Didn't say I wanted to trick you out in a lot of whim-whams," Lady Hollinwood interrupted, straightening the Henrietta ruff that surrounded her head like the nimbus of a saint. "Just because you're in mourning ain't any excuse to be behindhand in the mode. Besides, I won't have relations of mine running around looking like a couple of rustics. Why, just the thing to make me seem a regular shab. Well, what's the matter, child?" she asked impatiently. "Shouldn't you like some new clothes?"

"Oh, yes, ma'am," Athena said truthfully. "Only at the moment, you see—well, I'm afraid Mama and I have scarcely a feather to fly with."

"Thought so," her ladyship declared bluntly. "No cause to trouble yourself in that regard, child. Won't bother to detail the particulars, but I'm rather warm in the purse myself."

"You're very good, ma'am," Athena murmured, suppressing a wild urge to confess the true nature of the debt she might soon owe her unsuspecting aunt. "Should you truly enjoy helping me go off?" she inquired curiously after a moment.

"Depend on it, child. The thing is, this everlasting sitting around always puts me directly into the hips," Lady Hollinwood confided. "This way, I'll enjoy seeing you shine 'em all down." She smiled in anticipation. "I daresay you've a fair eye for color, haven't you, what with all this painting business."

"Yes, I daresay I do," Athena offered cautiously. Then, anxious to avoid further discussion of that topic, she rose, saying apologetically, "If you'll excuse me now, ma'am—"

"I beg your pardon, child. No doubt you're wanting your bed. Just leave it to me, my dear, and I promise you'll be on the town in no time."

"Oh, I very much hope that I shall!" Athena said fervently.

NO ONE WOULD TAKE ME for anything but a country mouse in this rig-out, Athena thought ruefully the following morning as she smoothed a gown of worn gray kerseymere over her hips.

Lady Hollinwood was clearly in agreement. After a brief appraisal of Athena's attire, her ladyship at once exclaimed in heartfelt accents, "How very fortunate that you should have arrived before the season has yet begun. I've just been looking over some color plates," she said somewhat more tactfully, indicating several copies of the *Lady's Magazine*, "and I feel certain we can contrive to dress you quite satisfactorily."

It was only a short while before Lady Hollinwood's guests were seated across from her in a smartly painted barouche, making their way toward Leicester Square and Mme. Quiette, dressmaker to Her Royal Highness, Princess Caroline.

Sinking happily into Mme. Quiette's splendid establishment—which boasted rich Aubusson carpets, gilded chairs and elaborate mirrors covering an entire wall—and into her capable hands, the party at last emerged several hours later to dispose themselves wearily on the plump cushions of the waiting carriage and pile a large number of bandboxes at their feet.

Athena, for her part, was speechless at finding herself the owner of a high-waisted walking dress of bottle-green cambric and a matching velvet pelisse—not to mention a half dress of bronze crape and a sarcenet evening gown. Her mother could now boast a breakfast dress trimmed in fluted muslin and a dove-gray silk embellished by several rosettes. And even her ladyship hadn't hesitated to bespeak a taffeta robe in a startling shade of Clarence blue and a plum-colored spencer in the new figured silk from France called kluteen.

The following day was spent in a similar manner, beginning with a visit to a milliner's shop. There the party settled on a Leghorn hat and a velvet cap each for Athena and Mrs. Lindsay and a toque turban of bronze tulle with an enormous plume for Lady Hollinwood. Some time was then allotted to visiting a linen draper's to select India muslins and silk bombazines to be made into garments by her ladyship's seamstress. A visit to a haberdasher's in order to choose ribbons was followed in quick succession by additional stops for slippers, gloves and other necessary items until Athena's head began to ache from guilt as much as from fatigue.

Upon their return to Grosvenor Square, Lady Hollinwood and Mrs. Lindsay promptly retired for a much-needed rest. Athena soon found she was too overwrought to sleep, however, and so after a while she rose and retrieved her painting box from its hiding place under her bed.

She ran her hands over its familiar worn wooden surface before slipping open the brass lock. Inside, the jumble of paints and chalks and brushes laid next to her precious packets of paper and drawings offered its usual comfort. When she was small, it had just as conveniently held the few toys she possessed. The box had always been hers alone whatever it contained, its presence a welcome invitation to enter the private world of her imagination.

Accordingly, she selected paper and crayons and settled herself on a pile of pillows beneath the window to sketch.

All the faces she had glimpsed on her few forays through London jostled for notice in her mind, and she started one sketch after another—a vomiting drunkard reeling from a tavern, a sweeper boy covered with sores and soot, Mme. Quiette deferentially pressing the merits of her most expensive creation. But the subject Athena kept coming back to was the girl who had stared into their chaise, dumbly cradling her baby.

She continued to sketch steadily for close on two hours until, reaching blindly for a fresh sheet of paper, her hand met the bare wood of the box instead.

Racking her brain for a means by which she might obtain more sketching paper proved fruitless, so Athena was glad to set her worries aside when the time came to dress for tea.

She was beginning to feel thoroughly bored by the tea-time conversation and ready to withdraw, when a chance remark saved her.

"I do find Miss Austen's works so entertaining, don't you?" Mrs. Lindsay said shyly. "I believe her publisher has just brought out a posthumous book of hers. In Kent I don't see a new book for upwards of a year after it is issued."

At once Athena caught this lifeline. "There must be a bookseller hereabouts who could supply the volume immediately."

"I warrant Hatchard's in Piccadilly could," Lady Hollinwood observed. Then noting the questioning glance that Mrs. Lindsay cast her way, she waved her arm in a gesture of largesse. "Take the carriage, child, if you mean to go. I shan't be needing it. I fancy my coachman will know the direction well enough."

Having produced the desired result, Athena ran upstairs to don her new bonnet and pelisse. The carriage was soon brought to the door, and settling uneasily against the cushions, she summoned to mind the name of the only art shop in London with which she was at all familiar.

"Ackermann's, if you please," she said resolutely. "In the Strand."

CHAPTER TWO

AT PRECISELY THE MOMENT when Lady Hollinwood and her guests were sitting down to tea, the Honorable Giles Wescott strode purposefully into Ackermann's Repository of Art. His entrance elicited little reaction from the clients of that establishment, who merely noted the arrival of a tallish gentleman with an arresting, if not actually handsome, face, dressed in a refined manner.

Closer examination revealed a pair of piercing blue eyes, an aquiline nose, a nicely proportioned head of thick dark hair and a decidedly full mouth surmounting a well-muscled frame dressed in garments that could have issued only from the very best clothiers. But he was neither a nonpareil nor a veritable dash. Even his closest acquaintances had never been able satisfactorily to categorize him.

Although his coat was tailored by Weston and his Hessian boots provided by Hoby, the absence of an immoderately high shirt collar and striped silk waistcoat eliminated the possibility that Mr. Wescott was a Bond Street beau. He'd never been sighted tooling his phaeton recklessly through the city streets or challenging another to best his time to Oxford, so he was no blood, but he was a notable whip, maintained an enviable stable and was always well up with the hounds. While he enjoyed donning the gloves in Jackson's Saloon and gambling at White's, he was equally comfortable circling the dance-floor at Almack's and discussing the latest political intrigues at Brooks's. Yet his addiction to art and a collection said to be the envy of rival connoisseurs saved him from being a mere Corinthian and leading a completely casual existence.

It was the pursuit of his artistic appetites that had today brought Giles to 101 Strand, there to describe his latest purchases to the proprietor, Rudolf Ackermann. Giles had returned only a week ago from a leisurely and productive tour of the Continent, during which he'd acquired a small but pleasing Tintoretto, a portrait by Rembrandt and an impressive statue by Cellini. Naturally he had hastened to resume a long-standing custom of sharing with Mr. Ackermann his impressions of the art world abroad, formed when they had first met some five years earlier at Christie's Auction Rooms.

For Ackermann's was indeed far more than a shop offering art materials. Starting out as a publisher with a modest printing establishment, Ackermann had opened the shop as a means of peddling the carefully prepared editions in which he specialized, these being, for the most part, handsomely etched in the new aquatint method recently introduced from France. But though Ackermann proclaimed that he was ever receptive to new techniques, he was known to prefer the

services of such fashionable illustrators as Rowlandson rather than risk taking a flier on any of the newer
artists who constantly besieged him in the hope of securing a commission. This reluctance to break new
ground had often been the cause of spirited argu-
ments between him and Giles Wescott.

Giles was curious, therefore, to discover Ackermann's reaction to a work he'd acquired by an exper-
imental Spanish painter named Francisco Goya, who
was still little heralded outside his own country. He
was consequently disappointed to be informed that the
publisher was already engaged but would be available
shortly. However, the delivery of a fresh supply of
watercolor cakes soon served to distract his attention.
Welcoming some physical labor after several months
of doing nothing but climbing in and out of his traveling chaise, he promptly stripped off his coat and began to unpack the crates with enthusiasm.

Thus it was understandable that Athena, entering
Ackermann's a few minutes later and seeing before her
a man in shirt-sleeves and plain trousers working behind a counter, should mistake the Honorable Giles
Wescott for a shop assistant.

Overawed by the wealth of materials around her, she
stood hesitantly by the counter, hoping her presence
would be noticed.

At last, however, conscious of her aunt and mother
waiting at home, she cleared her throat. "I beg your
pardon," she began diffidently. "Please bring me
some paper suitable for crayon drawings."

On looking up and encountering the earnest gaze of a modishly attired young lady, Giles was snared by a sense of humor that had more than once landed him in the basket and which, in consequence, he was usually at great pains to conceal. He couldn't resist making the most of the absurd situation in which he now found himself.

"For yourself, miss?" he inquired in what he hoped was an appropriately servile tone, lounging against the counter. He favored his customer with a brashly admiring smile.

"Yes, of course," Athena said in surprise, recollecting too late that ladies of quality would be likely to leave such purchases to their drawing master. "I'm an artist, you see. That is to say, I hope I shall be one," she amended conscientiously.

"Indeed," Giles acknowledged politely, his interest engaged by a lady who openly aspired to a state that others of his acquaintance would deem quite unfashionable, if not positively unseemly. Delicately, he endeavored to probe further. "You draw a little then, I take it? And also, perchance, engage in the decorative arts, as well? So many ladies find satisfaction in painting on china or doing japanwork and the like."

"Yes, I've heard that the desire to embellish every surface threatens to become a veritable craze," Athena said thoughtfully. "But I fancy I should find such work a bore," she confided.

"Oh, should you?" Giles asked in a sympathetic tone.

"Certainly. Though decorating screens might well please those who indulge in art as a mere hobby-horse—which, I should tell you, I do not—and who haven't been encouraged to pursue a more worthwhile object." She paused to adjust the unaccustomed weight of her new hat.

"As you have been—?" Giles prompted, reluctant to leave off now that the conversation had taken such an intriguing turn.

"Not precisely," Athena admitted with a tiny smile. Then, flattered by the solicitous interest of this most superior clerk, she elaborated. "My abilities have been fostered to a certain degree, out of necessity, so that I might assist my father in his studio. He was an artist. Roderick Lindsay—?" She regarded her companion hopefully.

"Indeed?" he said again politely. "I fear I'm not acquainted with his work."

"Well, there's really not the least reason why you should be," Athena said frankly. "We're from Kent, after all. But you see, my father having recently stuck his spoon in the wall, Mama and I determined to come to town for a while to stay with my aunt."

Highly amused by this brisk manner of referring to one of the most delicate of life's events, Giles managed, albeit with some difficulty, to refrain from laughing. "I see," he said in a bland voice. "Your first visit? Then I trust you're enjoying a few of the sights."

"No!" Athena declared emphatically before recollecting where she was and continuing in a more moderate tone. "I daresay I should enjoy them, of course, if I had the opportunity to do so. However, to date the only sights I've seen are the interiors of well-nigh every dressmaker's and milliner's shop in London.''

Giles couldn't repress an appreciative smile at these remarks. "I take it, then,'' he inquired sympathetically, staring in a pointed way at his companion's head, "that you aren't one of those ladies consumed by an interest in fashion.''

"Oh, I confess to an interest, to be sure,'' Athena said, rolling her eyes up at the large brim of her hat. "However, it isn't a positive passion for me as it is for my aunt.''

Giles, likewise gifted with a relative whose whole existence revolved around the latest visit to her dressmaker, finally laughed out loud. "But I confess I find myself at a loss,'' he admitted after a moment. "If you haven't come to study the styles or to pay homage to our places of interest, then why have you come?''

"Why, so that I may learn how to paint!'' Athena exclaimed, as if the answer were patently obvious. "You see, although it's true that I've been painting for simply ages, I've never really had the opportunity to learn whether my efforts had any distinction or not. And then, too, there are still a great many things I don't know—the knack of working firsthand with a model, for example. You see, my subjects, although most obliging, were not inclined to remain stationary.'' Her eyes twinkled reflectively. "And you can't conceive how very tiresome it is to be obliged to move one's materials every few minutes in order to keep pace with one's chosen cow.''

Giles laughed again and was about to essay a further question when Athena, reminded by the conversation of the purpose of her trip, reminded him in turn of her request for drawing paper. A tactful conference with one of the legitimate shop clerks enabled him to fill the order, but he found himself loath to put an end to the interview. Whether this was due to the agreeable sensation of flirting with an outspoken young lady clearly not in the common mold or to a sincere desire to discover the nature of her artistic abilities, he couldn't have said for certain.

As Athena—paper safely in hand—turned to leave, he hurriedly blurted out without pausing to consider the consequences, "I'd be very pleased if you'd allow me to look at your drawings, miss. That is to say," he corrected himself hastily, "Mr. Ackermann does sometimes take an interest in unknown artists. And we assistants are enjoined to be on the lookout for new talent," he improvised, pushing aside any momentary discomfort caused by the dubious nature of these inventions.

Athena, whose progress toward the door had been abruptly checked by this unexpected vision of so effortlessly achieving her ambition, took a deep breath and resolved to proceed with caution. "Pray, do not quiz me, sir," she said slowly. "I assure you I am as yet the merest amateur. Why should Mr. Ackermann wish to see my work?"

Recklessly casting about for a means of persuading this suddenly prudent miss to enter into his plans, Giles seized on a more realistic tack. "I believe that

drawings of high quality may be placed for sale here."
He stopped, but feeling altogether enchanted by the
afternoon's events, he couldn't resist adding a further
inducement. "And then, too," he continued, though
now he knew that what he said was entirely untrue,
"there always remains the possibility of obtaining a
commission to illustrate one of the many volumes Mr.
Ackermann publishes. Perhaps you're acquainted with
the *Microcosm of London*, which he brought out
some years back?"

"Oh, yes!" Athena breathed. "A neighbor of ours
possessed all three volumes and was kind enough to
make them available to me on occasion. You don't
think— Do you truly believe I might be so fortunate—?"

"Of course, I couldn't say," Giles inserted truthfully. "I can't promise, you know, but if you were to
return, say, tomorrow with several of your drawings,
I'd do my best to see them presented in a favorable
light to Mr. Ackermann. You do have a few that are
of something other than cows?" he inquired anxiously.

"Oh, yes," Athena assured him, already happily
beginning to mull over the inventory of her painting
box.

"Excellent!" Giles escorted her to the door of the
shop. "We're agreed, then—tomorrow afternoon,
without fail?" He bowed the visitor out, barely closing the door before starting to wonder why he'd chosen to become enmeshed in such a tangled coil and

whether his publisher friend would enjoy the role he was to play in the whole smoky business.

Turning away from the entrance, he beheld Ackermann himself standing a few feet away and giving every evidence of deriving a good deal of satisfaction from the maneuverings of his newest gentleman-in-waiting.

Unsure of how much Ackermann had witnessed but mindful of Gentleman Jackson's advice that a strong offense is the quickest way to gain the advantage of an opponent, Giles at once seized the initiative. "Dash it, man, don't go sneaking up on a fellow like that!" he complained, crossing the room to retrieve his coat. "You gave me quite a turn, I assure you." He flicked a nonexistent piece of dust from his trousers.

Indicating that they should remove to his private office, Ackermann blandly observed, "Appears to me that you're the one who's been doing the sneaking, dear fellow. You should have told me you were longing for a taste of the shop. Though I should tell you that we shopkeepers don't commonly entertain our bits of game during business hours."

"Oh, gammon! Anyone with a proper pair of saucers can see she's no light-skirt." Giles favored his companion with a disgusted look.

"Don't doubt as you're more conversant with these matters than I," Ackermann said mildly.

Ignoring this jab, Giles perched casually on the edge of the huge mahogany table that served as his friend's desk. "The thing is," he admitted, having decided to tackle the problem in a straightforward manner, "the lady's an artist. What's more, I told her you'd be glad to look at a few of her sketches.''

"You told her what?" Ackermann demanded incredulously. "Are you trying to roast me?" Remembering that it wouldn't serve to land on the wrong side of a very valuable acquaintance, he continued more judiciously. "Truly, I don't mind a whit if you choose to play handy-dandy with some female or other, dear boy. I won't rumble your lay—besides, dashed if I know what it is—but you know perfectly well I don't have any truck with lady painters."

"You engaged Maria Hadfield to illustrate those verses by Perdita Robinson," Giles protested.

"Good business," Ackermann explained briefly. "Married to Cosway, and he ain't an artist to scoff at. Then, too, our Prince appeared quite smitten by the beauteous Miss Robinson—and where he leads, others follow. Not the same thing at all," he pointed out. "Still, there's a bit of soft to be made by chits who are handy with a brush. Devilishly clever at simple things, most of 'em." He considered an aquatint hanging on his wall for a moment before adding generously, "And once in a while, maybe, there's a girl with a fair eye and a steady hand who can do a passable copy when I want one. But at any rate, don't believe I caught the lady's name?"

"Her father's Roderick Lindsay, the artist," Giles replied enthusiastically. "The lady's new to town, I understand. Staying with her aunt."

"Really? Whereabouts?" Seeing from his friend's rueful expression that he was at a stand, Ackermann indulged in a hearty laugh. "It appears you ain't the only one who's playing deep," he observed after catching his breath. "Exactly what the devil is your interest in this lady, anyway?"

"Since the lady's a painter and I'm a collector, it only stands to reason that I'd welcome the chance to discover a new protégé," Giles invented, neatly side-stepping the heart of the matter. "What's more, I fancy that wouldn't do you a speck of harm either."

"Poppycock!" Ackermann exclaimed inelegantly. "You never could tell a proper whisker, if that's what all this is. Well, if you don't mean to say, it's all the same to me. I wash my hands of the whole crack-brained thing." Then, feeling obliged, after all, to enter a warning, he added, "No doubt you'll spike your own guns, but that's your affair. Go ahead by all means, my dear fellow; just don't come crying to me to pay the shot."

Although somewhat offended by the intimation that a gentleman of close on forty should need to depend on someone else to steer him past the rapids, Giles accepted the offer of a truce with evident good humor. He then partook generously of the very fine Madeira Ackermann supplied to distinguished visitors and proffered, in return, an enameled snuffbox.

"Now then, Wescott," Ackermann coaxed, "tell me about your travels."

HER ARRIVAL had clearly interrupted a discussion of some consequence, Athena decided, as she crossed the drawing room toward her relatives. Removing her hat with a flourish, she sketched a curtsy before her mother. Then she held out a handsome, leather-bound copy of *Northanger Abbey* with a smile, saying, "Here is the lending library come to visit you in person."

Noting her niece's flushed cheeks, Lady Hollinwood observed first, "Must say your outing seems to have agreed with you no end, child. But come, pull up a chair and let us tell you what we've been plotting the while."

"Only consider, love," Mrs. Lindsay burst out excitedly in turn, "Louisa has been so gracious as to offer to hold a party in our honor!"

"Entirely unexceptional, my dear," Athena's aunt assured her hastily, one hand stealing up to pat her steel-gray curls. "Merely to introduce you both to a few of my friends. We'll require some simple entertainment—perhaps a little music. Major Stebbing can bring Elizabeth. His daughter, you know, and a most accomplished student of the pianoforte. Such a prettily behaved child. I do hope you two will like each other. She's a trifle younger than you; just turned eighteen, I believe.

"Now, let's see," she continued. "I'll have the Merivales and their girl Fanny, and the Laverstokes and their daughters, and a couple of young men to start with. But no dancing. One or two tables for cards—nothing boisterous like lottery tickets, but maybe whist. And ices and cakes and lemonade. Champagne? No, too vulgar."

Deliberations concerning the party continued throughout dinner. Athena soon found herself paying less attention to the particulars and more to how the progress of the discussion seemed to complement that of the meal. A genial dissection of the guest list engaged them during the oysters fried in batter. This was followed by a lengthy contemplation of an appropriate menu—with the crimped cod and boiled leg of lamb. A digression into the recreations to be offered accompanied the side dishes of green goose and cutlets in wine sauce. And the arrival of a curd pudding coincided with a review of the necessary preparations.

"Splendid!" her ladyship exclaimed at last, bringing Athena back to her surroundings with a jolt. "I warrant that will serve quite nicely," she said with satisfaction, rising to adjourn to the drawing room. There, Athena endured another quarter hour of small talk with fortitude before pleading fatigue from her afternoon excursion and being excused to seek her bed.

Once she'd secured the door, however, Athena brought out her painting box and extracted from it a thick pile of drawings. Then, settling down on the floor near the fireplace, she proceeded to examine each sketch in turn with the aid of this gentle light, applying to her work the severely critical eye that she imagined Ackermann would employ. But the closer she looked, the more inadequate and amateur she felt the sketches to be. The colors in this landscape were too muddy, and the composition of that one decidedly unbalanced. Another, though delicately wrought, was finished by a less than steady hand, and a fourth bore all the marks of haste.

Athena progressed slowly through the stack until every drawing had been allotted a fair review and the fire had been reduced to a mass of embers. The result of this scrutiny, a slender sheaf of a dozen sketches, offered her little encouragement.

For one thing, she decided, pressing her fingers against her aching eyes, the pieces were too small, most of them scarcely the equal of a good-sized book. *But I could only take a very little bit of paper,* she argued silently, *or it would have been missed, so one sheet had to serve for two drawings.* Then, too, her palette did appear sadly limited. *Surely I could have contrived to obtain more than stubs of crayons and remnants of watercolor cakes,* she said to herself—and then halted abruptly. *Why, I'm entirely too busy making excuses for my work,* she realized in surprise. *Other artists must have labored under a greater handicap than I and still produced good pictures. And I can't, after all, stand beside my drawings and explain, "On that day I'd already painted ten hours in my father's studio, so I beg pardon if my stroke wasn't firm."*

No, she decided, inadequate or not, her paintings alone would have to speak for her ability. She'd consider herself a poor artist indeed if they could not.

This introspection having fortified her somewhat for the trial ahead, she replaced the painting box in its hidey-hole and carefully laid the chosen drawings on a shelf in the wardrobe. Then, hastily changing into her nightdress, she slipped into the warmth of the bed and prepared for sleep—only to be brought up short again by the realization that she'd not yet considered how she was to get to Ackermann's the next day.

Oh, well, I daresay tomorrow shall be soon enough to discover if I'm as clever as I'm sometimes accounted to be, she thought tiredly, wriggling deeper into her quilts, and forthwith fell asleep.

THE NEXT MORNING, the household was astir at an early hour. Before she'd even finished dressing, Athena could detect the muffled sounds of feet moving rapidly up and down the stairs in response, she guessed, to instructions issued by her aunt.

And indeed, there were a sufficient number of tasks to occupy family and staff alike for the better part of the day. Since Lady Hollinwood devoted herself to composing the invitations, much of the remaining work devolved upon her relatives. Mrs. Lindsay was persuaded to direct Scorsby in the cleaning of the ballroom, and Athena found herself put to designing floral arrangements to grace the refreshment tables and sundry corners of the room.

These pursuits having easily consumed the whole of the morning, it was well past noon when the three ladies assembled in the dining room to partake of a cold collation and relate the progress each had made in her particular realm. Mrs. Lindsay's efforts were promptly applauded. The simple sketches Athena had conceived to present her ideas were also immediately ac-

cepted, although her aunt was heard to mutter that it
was a foolish waste of time to draw pictures of posies
that would only last a few hours. Lady Hollinwood
then withdrew to conduct yet another interview with
Cook, and Mrs. Lindsay excused herself to return to
the ballroom. Athena made her way slowly upstairs to
her room, there to consider how she might manage to
pay a visit to Ackermann's before the end of the
afternoon.

She was just concluding that her lovely pink-and-
white bedchamber—indeed, her new home—must be
nothing but an elegant prison if she was forever trying
to escape it when Lady Hollinwood thrust open the
door.

"I wonder if you'd agree to execute a few errands
for me, child?" she inquired anxiously without
preamble. "There's no one I can spare with sense
enough to get the things done right, and I warrant Meg
wouldn't feel easy gadding about by herself as you
seem to, even if I was thick-witted enough to send her.
Beg pardon, I'm sure, but all this fiddle-faddle makes
me a trifle cross. We've still to order the flowers, and
then there are the fruit ices to bespeak at Gunther's,
and . . . I've written a list." She regarded her niece
hopefully.

With a reassuring smile, Athena plucked the paper
from her aunt's hand and waited till she had bustled
away in a swirl of skirts. Then, retrieving her drawings, she stuffed them inside her old pelisse, jammed
on a faded black straw hat and tripped hastily down
to the carriage.

The drive to Ackermann's was accomplished altogether too quickly. Athena was uncomfortably aware of a shortness of breath and a constriction about her chest that she hadn't experienced since the age of ten, when she'd first pointed her pony at a hedge and seen the hedge rushing inexorably to meet her. It was with great relief, therefore, that she located the man with whom she'd made the appointment directly inside the door of the shop, patiently awaiting her arrival.

To be truthful, Giles was feeling anything but patient. Mindful that he'd neglected to fix a time for the interview, he'd awakened early, distinctly out of sorts with the world and irritated by the prospect of being forced to dangle around Ackermann's all afternoon until the young lady arrived, if indeed she ever did. And thus it was with at least an equal sense of relief that he finally saw her come in. Bowing politely, he escorted her to a quiet corner set with two convenient armchairs in which visitors were encouraged to rest from the day's exertions.

Because this was the first time she'd ever given her work over for serious review, Athena was ill acquainted with how an exchange of this sort was usually conducted. Once he'd accepted the sketches from her shaky hand, her companion commenced turning them over slowly one by one in complete silence. But although the silence was scarcely calculated to set her mind at ease, she was comforted by the reminder that it was not this man's good opinion as much as that of Ackermann that she desired. She was so distracted by wondering whether it was preferable to affect complete lack of interest rather than betray by some comment the extent to which she felt her future rested on the outcome of today's interview that Giles's first words took her by surprise.

"Now that's a different proposition entirely!" he exclaimed ambiguously. He held up a likeness of Mme. Quiette, complete with deferential shop assistants, and then regarded it fixedly for some moments. "Miss Lindsay, is it? Well, your landscapes are certainly not to be faulted, though I fear there are many who are proficient in that genre. But this, now, is a trifle more unusual," he continued, nodding at the sketch in his hand. "I apprehend it must be one of the many shops you mentioned visiting the other day," he said, his eyes twinkling.

Without further prompting, Athena found herself retelling the whole of the visit to Mme. Quiette's. "And the proprietress would let my aunt purchase the most unflattering gown," she concluded, "merely to avoid offending such a valuable patron and to keep her business, I suppose."

Well acquainted with toadies who preyed on members of the upper class, Giles nodded. "Indeed. And if I may say so, you've captured her avarice most admirably: the craftly expression in the eyes, the obsequious bow. Yes, complete to a shade—and very nearly libelous, too, I imagine." Athena glanced apprehensively at a fashionable lady entertaining her little son with a book of prints. "But no more so, of course, than any of Rowlandson's drawings, or those of the Cruikshanks," he hastened to reassure her.

"And satire ain't a hanging crime, after all." He held the drawing out at arm's length for a moment and then said thoughtfully, "It's a pity this wasn't done in oils, though. You have worked in that medium, have you not?"

"Oh, yes," Athena admitted, "only my present situation doesn't encourage—doesn't allow me room to set up a proper space to work."

"I see," Giles said politely. "How unfortunate." He wondered if it might be inadvisable to probe further. "Now that I think of it, I have heard that lady painters frequently encounter unusual difficulty in securing studios of their own." He offered her the warm smile that had encouraged more than one unsuspecting listener to give up a certified confidence.

But if she was as yet unused to the ways of society, Athena could never be accused of being slow in matters involving one's wits. Though a certain curiosity about her identity was understandable and indeed to be expected, she wasn't such a babe that she failed to deduce that the current line of questioning was intended to extract some clue to her address.

"Oh, do you know very many lady painters, then?" she inquired, widening her eyes innocently. "I confess I hadn't thought to find a shop assistant so very well informed."

"But we're so much more valuable to our customers if we strive to keep abreast of the times, don't you agree?" Then, observing that his companion was beginning to draw on her gloves, Giles continued smoothly without waiting for a reply. "Allow me to assure you that I'll endeavor to present your delightful drawings to Mr. Ackermann without delay. Perhaps you might furnish me with your direction so that I may see to their safe return.''

"Pray don't trouble yourself, sir," Athena parried. "It would be far more convenient if I were to stop back sometime next week to inquire what progress has been made.''

Left with nothing to do but graciously admit defeat, Giles escorted his visitor to the door of the shop and watched her climb into the stylish rig that awaited her. As he turned away, he had to confess that he was no closer to learning the whereabouts of this enigmatic young lady than he had been the day before. What's more, he might now be obliged to spend every hour of the following week dancing attendance at Ackermann's if he was indeed bent on finding out who she was.

Promptly determining that he was in need of a strong restorative, he shoved the drawings into his coat pocket and strode outside. Hailing the first passing hack, he jumped in and ordered the jehu seated on the box, "White's—and spring 'em, man!"

CHAPTER THREE

A SHORT WHILE LATER the hack careened into St. James's Street and quivered to a stop before the imposing edifice of one of the most fashionable clubs in London. But before he'd even reached the door, Giles heard himself loudly hailed by a figure gesturing wildly at him from the bow window where Beau Brummell had formerly held court.

Once inside the club, he saw the person in question, his closest friend, the Honorable Reginald Thurston, advancing to greet him. With practiced, mincing steps, Mr. Thurston described a precisely straight line across the room—compelled to do so by collar points extending well above his jaw and held tightly in place by a starched cravat, arranged in the severe folds of the Oriental, which restricted his head from turning more than one degree to the right or left. His hair was cunningly disordered in the windswept style. An enormous diamond tiepin glittered on his chest above a waistcoat that was nearly blinding in its embroidered splendor. A long-tailed coat of black superfine, wrought by a master hand, surmounted a pair of skintight pantaloons in canary yellow.

His friend having at last reached his side, Giles smiled at him fondly and inquired in a polite tone, "Did you wish to speak with me about something in particular, Reggie, or were you simply enjoying a bit of exercise by waving your arms like a looby?"

"Where have you been, my dear fellow?" Reginald complained. "Went by your lodgings yesterday and this afternoon and damned if your man didn't know where you'd gone or when you'd return."

"Oh, just on the toddle, you know. Don't fancy that I must keep you apprised of my every movement."

"Not at all, dear boy, quite right," Reginald corrected himself hastily. "Only if you've not been to your rooms, you ain't heard yet about Lady Hollinwood's assemblage. Got an invitation myself this morning. Should think you're bound to have one, too."

"Now surely you don't mean to drag me to another of that old tabby's insipid affairs."

"Don't doubt that Fanny Merivale will be there, dear boy. Her mama and Lady Hollinwood are as tight as two doves in a coop. She's a rather pretty little thing, don't you think?"

"That may be true," Giles allowed. "But if the divine Miss Merivale has ever willingly let a single serious thought enter her charming head, I've yet to discover it."

"Ain't forgetting your father's instructions, are you, Giles?" Reginald inquired with more persistence than tact.

Forgetting was scarcely likely, Giles thought gloomily, given that his elderly parent, having recently lost patience with what he termed the nomadic existence of his only son, had sternly warned him to remedy the situation at once or incur his extreme displeasure. The beauteous Fanny Merivale—of impeccable lineage and no less impressive fortune—had been one of several young ladies recommended by Lord Wescott as worthy of his son's immediate attention.

Although he was not dependent on his father's goodwill for his income, Giles recognized his duty to marry and ensure that the family name would continue. Indeed, he'd set out obediently to find a wife, albeit not without first privately telling Reginald that—duty be hanged—he wouldn't be forced into marriage if his sentiments weren't engaged, as well.

Since Reginald had generously set aside his oft-expressed dislike of the wedded state so as to assist him, Giles tempered his response accordingly.

"How the deuce could I forget?" he exclaimed, ruffling his hair until he looked as if he'd just emerged from a whirlwind. "Oh, dash it—I suppose we must attend the cursed thing, after all. But I warn you, I shan't stand about champing at the bit if you get hooked up with one of her ladyship's interminable card games."

"Just as you wish, dear fellow," Reginald agreed at once. "Promise we won't even stay above a half hour, if you like."

THE HOURS SPENT PREPARING for the party had slipped by, Athena noted with surprise, even though from the moment she had left her drawings at Ackermann's, she had felt like a bird seeing her fledglings take wing for the first time. She was grateful to be able to place herself now in the capable hands of Malings, her aunt's dresser, and happily to find her confidence fully justified when she turned at last to regard herself in the mirror.

There she beheld the reflection of a tall and unexpectedly attractive stranger attired in a stylish gown of moss-green sarcenet. The low neckline set off her creamy skin to perfection. Her dark hair had been twisted into a high knot and parted in front to allow a few careful ringlets to fall in studied disarray over her ears. Around her neck was the single strand of pearls her father had presented to her on her twenty-first birthday. A white lace shawl was draped around her shoulders to ward off the evening chill, and dainty slippers of Denmark satin peeped from beneath the hem of her gown.

Clearly she wasn't the only one, however, who'd made good use of her time. Mrs. Lindsay presented a charming picture in the dove-gray silk set off by her sister-in-law's cashmere shawl and a handsome emerald pendant that had been her mother's. And Lady Hollinwood's costume—a shocking-puce robe trimmed with puffings of reversed satin and ornamented by a half-dozen bracelets, several necklaces and an enormously ugly pair of earrings—was undeniably arresting, as her niece amusedly guessed she had intended it should be.

Even the ballroom appeared properly primed for the evening. Hundreds of candles drew prisms of color from the newly polished chandeliers. Enormous vases of showy white lilies and delicate lilacs softened the corners. And bowls of deep purple irises and golden marigolds graced refreshment tables loaded with enough delicacies to tempt the discriminating palates of her ladyship's guests.

Not unexpectedly, Athena noted, the first of these proved to be the Major Stebbing to whom her aunt had often referred. He moved across the ballroom as quickly as possible, given the impediment presented by a stiffened left leg. The leg was a souvenir from Toulouse, the battle that had taken the life of his friend Gerald Hollinwood and subsequently forced him to retire from active service. Since then, he'd adhered with great reluctance to the dictates of his pocketbook but rather more cheerfully to his promise to look after Gerald's wife. Once he'd made the happy discovery that they shared an inordinate taste for gossip, scarcely three days had passed when he'd failed to present himself for a leisurely prose.

The major was towing in his wake a diminutive blonde dressed in cerulean crape whom Athena at once guessed to be his daughter Elizabeth. Upon being introduced, the young lady looked shyly up at her and said in a barely audible voice, "Oh, my father has told me all about you, Miss Lindsay."

This innocent statement was sufficient to cause the speaker's cheeks to color furiously. Her embarrassment promptly won her an immediate place in Athena's heart, and gently drawing her aside, she endeavored to put Elizabeth at ease by admiring her gown.

"Do you like it?" Elizabeth whispered at last, after Athena had nearly despaired of a response. "Indeed, I believe the color is all the crack." She stood silent for a while before blurting out, "Doubtless you're aware that looks such as mine are very much the fashion, only as soon as I'm forced to open my mouth the illusion is broken. I very much dislike large social gatherings, you see, and would like never to go to another party again. Papa becomes quite cross with my unfortunate lack of address, which you can't have failed to notice...." Elizabeth dipped her head at this admission and focused her attention on irretrievably ruining the bow in her white satin sash.

Athena was just about to make a sympathetic response when the major hove into view.

"Well, well, m'dears! Taken to each other like a pair of hunters to the fences?" he exclaimed in a hearty voice. "Just the thing my little Beth needs, I warrant. Too shy by half, you know," he confided to Athena with a lamentable want of tact. "Always pounding on that infernal instrument of hers. Far better, I'm thinking, to get out and about and learn how to speechify a bit in public."

"Then I should tell you, sir," Athena interposed quickly, moved by her new friend's painful blushes, "that we two mean to spend a great deal of time in each other's pockets from now on, do we not?'' She cast an encouraging smile at Elizabeth and was promptly rewarded by a grateful one in return.

"Capital!'' the major declared.

While the season hadn't yet officially begun and London was consequently rather thin of company, everyone of note who had arrived in town had been invited to Lady Hollinwood's gathering. Though the evening wasn't very far advanced, the ballroom was already so crowded that Athena's view of the door had long since been obscured. It was mere chance that a break in the crowd occurred just at the moment when she looked to see how her mother and aunt were faring and she was afforded an unobstructed glimpse of an oddly familiar figure, impeccably attired in evening dress, entering the room.

She had to be mistaken, she told herself, blinking rapidly. What would a shop assistant be doing at her aunt's party—and dressed like a gentleman besides? No, the resemblance was only a coincidence. Hadn't she once heard an itinerant mystic tell her father that everyone had a double somewhere in the world?

She was on the point of asking Elizabeth if she knew who the newest arrival was when her aunt sailed across the room toward her, the gentleman in question and another in tow. The closer they got, the more dreadfully clear it became to Athena that her first conclusion hadn't been wrong, after all. This was no imaginary twin but the selfsame individual to whom she'd so recently confided her most private dreams.

Not once but twice she had taken him for an insignificant clerk. Her mortification was surpassed only by her anger at having been deceived by a man who was clearly known to the very cream of polite society.

She did, however, derive a fleeting satisfaction from his own reaction once he saw his destination. He gave a start, and then an expression of guilt—with perhaps a touch of regret?—flashed across his face. Nevertheless, to Athena's eyes he seemed to have recovered his composure with masterful ease by the time the trio had arrived and Lady Hollinwood had made the introductions.

"Mr. Giles Wescott, Mr. Reginald Thurston—I believe you're already on the nod with Major Stebbing and his daughter, Elizabeth. Allow me, then, to present my niece, Miss Athena Lindsay, who's agreed to make her home here with me for a bit," her ladyship said in what Athena felt to be an odiously ingratiating tone.

"Servant, Miss Lindsay," Reginald said politely.

"Servant," Giles echoed with a graceful bow.

"Wasn't there a hermit by the name of Giles in the seventh century?" Athena inquired in a thoughtful tone. "The patron saint of cripples, I believe."

"Quite so," Giles agreed dryly. "Though I hadn't the least notion that a young lady of your station would be so astonishingly knowledgeable."

"Oh, I'm a veritable repository of information, I assure you," Athena declared with a wave of her hand. "Names, dates and faces are all meat and drink to me."

"How very commendable," Giles replied in a bland voice.

Lady Hollinwood, having witnessed this exchange with evident satisfaction, abruptly recollected her duties. Turning toward Elizabeth with an inviting smile, she inquired, "I wonder if you'd consent to play a few tunes for us now, my dear? Doubtless we'd all enjoy a little diversion."

Athena shortly found herself inconveniently seated between Major Stebbing and Giles Wescott in a row of gilt chairs drawn up along the far side of the ballroom facing the pianoforte. Her unease in being placed next to Giles was rapidly replaced by a sincere apprehension for her new friend as she watched Elizabeth sit down at the pianoforte and raise her hands to begin. But the first strains of a Mozart sonata were rendered with a steady and expressive touch.

No sooner had she relaxed in her chair than Giles leaned over to whisper in what she thought was a most condescending way, "You needn't have worried, you know. Miss Stebbing may often seem at a loss in social settings but never in her playing. But then, I find first impressions so frequently deceiving, don't you agree?"

Athena fixed her eyes on Elizabeth. "Decidedly!" she said feelingly under her breath, "though I must say you appear to have vastly more experience in that arena than I, sir."

"A veritable hit," he replied appreciatively in an undertone. "But I never intended to fool you for long."

"Oh, what a lie!" Athena whispered scornfully, making a futile attempt to check the angry color that mounted to her cheeks. "When I think of how shabbily you've twice behaved, it puts me quite out of patience."

"But surely you don't mean to have a turn-up with me here," Giles murmured. "Only consider what a spectacle we should make."

"Oh!" she gasped, stung into an unladylike desire to spin around and box his ears. "To think that you should lecture me about appearances when all the time it is you who has been suspect in your conduct."

"Undoubtedly," Giles agreed readily, much to her confusion. "Though how inelegant of you to say so. But perhaps we'd be well advised to postpone this discussion until another time," he pointed out quietly. "I'll call on you tomorrow, if I may—when we'll no doubt both feel freer to come to fisticuffs." He leaned coolly back in his chair.

Reluctantly agreeing that she hadn't the slightest desire to call attention to their conversation, Athena lapsed into silence. It proved but a small consolation that Giles politely excused himself at the end of the concert to saunter across the room with his friend and join the laughing crowd assembled around a very dashing and high-spirited blonde who had been pointed out to her earlier as Lord Merivale's eldest daughter Fanny.

Thereafter, Athena applied herself to the task of drawing out the diffident Elizabeth Stebbing. Indeed, she scarcely noticed when Giles took his leave a quarter hour or so later, save to conclude that he'd no doubt removed to more profitable hunting grounds.

ATHENA'S FIRST RECOLLECTIONS as she lay in bed the next morning concerned her ill-fated encounter with Mr. Wescott. That she had relegated him to a role so far below his true place in the world was not important, she assured herself, drawing the quilt up to her chin. In any case, mere possession of a graceful figure and an engaging smile was not a fair indicator of a man's station.

The real source of her present chagrin, she admitted, was the unrepentant nature of his conduct at her aunt's party. Athena folded her hands behind her head and scowled at the bed curtains. If he'd appeared at all humbled, if he'd acknowledged that his actions had first misled and then humiliated her, she'd have been much more inclined to forgive his deception.

As it was, this dishonorable gentleman now held her future in his hands. And how could she be sure that he would guard her secret wish to become a serious artist? The prospect of her cherished ambition being disclosed to her scandalized aunt made her want to bury her head beneath the pillow.

Resolutely, Athena closed her mind to Giles Wescott and swung her legs out of bed.

WHEN SHE DESCENDED to the dining room a half hour later, Athena found Mrs. Lindsay already addressing a generous platter of cold beef. "I must say you appear in fine fettle this morning, Mama," she observed as she poured a cup of coffee. "Was my aunt's gathering to your liking, then?"

"Oh, indeed, love. Louisa's friends were of a piece the most kind and so considerate," Mrs. Lindsay said, selecting a roll and beginning absentmindedly to butter it and her fingers, as well. "Why, we've already received several invitations," she continued dreamily.

"And were you able to discover any of my aunt's acquaintances who might be thought in need of my artistic services?" Athena inquired.

"Yes," Mrs. Lindsay answered somewhat indistinctly, sucking a finger clean of butter. "Lord Merivale spoke of a daughter younger than his Fanny—such a nicely behaved girl, don't you think? And I believe the Laverstokes mentioned another daughter—Melissa, or was it Clarissa?—who's to make her come-out next year."

Athena smiled approvingly at her mother. "Then you've fared excellently well, ma'am," she assured her. "Even a Bow Street runner couldn't have managed any better."

"Have you considered, though, how you're to broach the idea of painting lessons to these individuals, my love?" Mrs. Lindsay ventured timidly.

"Not precisely," Athena admitted. "Though doubtless I'll be able to think of some shift or other by which to convince them," she added with a false bravado that would have been obvious to anyone but her mother.

"Oh, I've every confidence that you will, love. Still, I confess I truly don't feel easy about proceeding any further, and particularly not without Louisa's permission—"

"Permission for what?" Lady Hollinwood demanded as she swept inopportunely into the room.

"Why, to be sure," Athena said smoothly, laying a quelling hand on her mother's shoulder, "your consent to visit the Egyptian Galleries at Montague House. I'm told they're a sight no visitor to London should ignore."

"Humpf! Doubtless—if you're interested in such things," Lady Hollinwood allowed with a slight shudder. "Of course, if it's art talk you're wanting, you couldn't do better than apply to Giles Wescott," she added meaningfully.

"Indeed?" Athena said carelessly. She took a small sip of coffee. "Is he so knowledgeable about art?"

"Knowledgeable!" her ladyship sputtered. "Good God, child, the man is a renowned collector, don't you know—a connoisseur, if you like. I hear he's got more paintings than the prince regent himself. Got more rolls of soft, besides. Practically as rich as the Golden Ball, they say," she observed happily, forking a piece of beef into her mouth. "Though why he chooses to waste his money on such fribbles is hard to understand, to my way of thinking."

Athena, who had paled visibly on hearing this glowing description of the man she'd taken for a shop assistant, rallied enough to interject tartly, "Perhaps the gentleman has a fondness for pretty things."

Lady Hollinwood gave a sharp laugh. "That he does, my love, that he does. But even so, he ain't exactly a rake, even if he is the biggest catch on the marriage mart. I thought he paid you more than a trifling amount of attention last night," her ladyship observed, clearly gratified. "Still, I understand he's as good as promised to Fanny Merivale—at any rate, that's what she appears to think. But then, I daresay you might be able to offer her a bit of competition along those lines."

"I assure you I haven't the least intention of dashing Miss Merivale's hopes," Athena said feelingly. "Nevertheless," she added after a moment, "I believe Mr. Wescott did express a desire to call on us today."

"Ha!" her ladyship scoffed. "I was sure you wouldn't be behindhand for long. Not," she declared smugly, turning toward Mrs. Lindsay, "that I'd credit for a minute any woman claiming she's not interested in the man. But let me tell you what's more important, child: If Mr. Wescott chooses to take you up, then you'll shortly be first oars with everyone of consequence. On that you may depend."

IT WAS WITH DIFFERING reactions that Athena and her aunt greeted the announcement late that afternoon that Mr. Giles Wescott had indeed come to pay the promised call.

Advancing across the room with rare grace, he executed a faultless bow before Lady Hollinwood, and bending to kiss her proffered hand, said, "Allow me to felicitate you, my lady, on a most enjoyable evening." Producing a brilliant smile that quite transformed his countenance, he added smoothly, "I assure you I can't remember a more interesting entertainment. But then doubtless my pleasure is traceable in part to the presence of your charming relatives." He turned toward Athena, raising his eyebrows in a speaking way.

Lady Hollinwood, who'd listened to this speech with rather less than perfect understanding, now offered in a playful voice, "Just a country mouse, are you, puss? Well, never fear—you'll soon learn how to go on."

Smiling maliciously at his hostess's tactlessness as much as at Athena's evident embarrassment, Giles said suavely, "But my thanks, ma'am, for putting me in mind of the purpose of my visit. I believe I heard you say that your niece hasn't yet had the opportunity to venture far from home. I wonder whether I might have the pleasure of taking her for a turn in Hyde Park?"

Fully bent on encouraging the gentleman along those very lines, her ladyship responded with an inappropriately girlish titter. "Why, what a perfectly delightful idea," she gushed. "Just the thing to start her off right foot first." She made little shooing motions with her hands as if to propel her niece bodily out of the house.

Even someone as strong-minded as Athena was helpless to withstand the force of such enthusiasm. And in any case, she could hardly be so ungrateful as to engage in a public battle of wills with her aunt. Therefore, a few minutes later, she found herself being gently handed into a natty tilbury. The pair of matched chestnuts were clearly anxious to have their heads, and the carriage moved off without further delay.

A restrained silence was maintained by both parties until the carriage had gained the entrance to the park and had turned down one of the many drives charmingly edged by rows of spring blossoms. At last, feeling compelled to speak or risk being struck dumb as she imagined Burckhardt must have been on his first view of Rameses' temple, Athena began stiffly, "I must apologize for—" at exactly the same moment as Giles offered, "Allow me to—"

Both broke off abruptly.

"I must apologize for my aunt's behavior, sir," Athena repeated first, staring straight ahead. "It must be sadly obvious to everyone, I fear, that she's out to snare a husband for me. Unfortunately, your visit only served to encourage her scheme."

"Pray don't consider it further," Giles advised earnestly, in a somewhat awkward voice. "And at any rate, it's our encounter at Ackermann's that I wanted to discuss. You see, I'd simply dropped in to give him the latest news from the Continent. I hadn't any notion you'd take me for one of his lackeys, though I know I did very little to disabuse you of the idea then or later."

"But you did show him my drawings, as you said you would?" Athena inquired, turning toward him at last.

"Well, no, I didn't actually—"

"Why, fiddledeedee!" she exclaimed angrily. "I should have known that a care-for-nothing such as yourself wouldn't keep his word. It's beyond crediting that I was so completely taken in by your professed sincerity when it was clearly nothing but an act."

"The only act was my lamentable imitation of a shopkeeper, I assure you," Giles insisted. "I promise I fully meant to show Ackermann your sketches, only I'm afraid I already knew there wasn't any hope. I may as well tell you," he explained more gently, "that he has no great opinion of lady painters—or of ladies, either, if truth be told. I've never been able to sway him from the belief that paintings by women are inevitably of lesser consequence than those by men. And neither have I managed to convince him to make use of female artists for illustrating his editions."

"But you said—" Athena persisted.

"I know," he broke in. "But unfortunately Ackermann holds that artists of the female sex are suited only to executing copies or attractive trifles with which to ornament the house."

"Yes, I see," Athena said slowly, crumpling in her seat. "Still, I confess it's a puzzle to me why so many people appear to think so. But aren't you, too, of the same mind, then?" she asked curiously, despite herself.

"No," he said simply. "And even if I had been, my travels would certainly have taught me otherwise. Possibly you've heard of Rosalba Carriera or Élisabeth Vigée-Lebrun? No? Then perhaps our own Angelica Kauffmann? Their work is quite remarkable. I know, you see, because I'm accounted something of a collector," he explained, looking down for a moment in a surprisingly self-conscious way.

"I promise your drawings are quite safe," he continued. "You may redeem them whenever you like. Indeed, I now fear the only thing that can't be redeemed is my true value in your eyes," he concluded with a tragic smile.

Athena gave a reluctant laugh. "Oh, you'd best leave off your hangdog look, sir. It's not at all becoming, I assure you."

"Dear me, first too bold and now too meek. Shall I never get it right?" Giles complained. That remark drew another laugh from Athena, and encouraged by this response, he added winningly, "We're agreed on a truce, then, are we not?"

"Oh, very well," Athena conceded. "It's only that I can't abide the thought of anyone trying to bamboozle me. Not that it appears to have made the least difference in this case."

"I collect you're disappointed," Giles said with quick sympathy. "Still, there are other ways for you to achieve your object, you know—though perhaps a discussion of those would best be left to another time. And now," he continued in a professorial tone, "since we've frittered away our drive without attending to any of the sights, we must return tomorrow and discover if we can't improve on our performance." He offered her another disarming smile. "I'd very much like to, both to return your sketches and, I hope, to become better acquainted. Well, what do you say?''

Athena studied his blue eyes carefully and after deliberately hesitating, she observed, ''I say, sir, that I believe you're a bit of a rake, after all, despite what my aunt tells me. And yet, do you know, I've every confidence that I'll soon learn to get the better of you,'' she concluded, with a sly smile.

Giles was occupied for a time in turning the horses in the direction of Grosvenor Square. Then, looking down at Athena, he said at last in an appreciative voice, ''And I have very little doubt whatsoever that you will.''

CHAPTER FOUR

"BEG YOUR PARDON, Reggie," Giles said to his friend. He offered a vacant smile to an acquaintance at the next table before shuffling the cards for a hand of macao. Brooks was crowded with men he knew, but Giles had hardly acknowledged a soul all evening. "Afraid my mind's adrift tonight."

"Any sapskull could see that, dear fellow," Reginald agreed good-naturedly. "Just saying it appears you'd be well-advised to fix your interest with Miss Merivale before overlong, if you truly mean to do so. Must have observed that coxcomb Wetherford paying her an uncommon lot of notice at Lady Hollinwood's the other night."

"But the man is an earl, after all," Giles pointed out mildly as he dealt. "And I collect his title must do much to recommend him to the lady, since I may only hope to be a viscount someday."

"Won't be much of anything, dear boy, if your father gets wind of the fact that matters are still at a stand," Reginald said bluntly. "Damned if you exchanged more than two words with the Beauty all evening, yet you spent a great deal of time with Miss Lindsay. Miss Merivale ain't about to enjoy being cut out like that. Thing is,'' he added penitently by way of explanation, ''be obliged to call myself a backfriend if I didn't try to bring you up to the mark. Promised I would, you know.''

''Yes, Reggie, and I fancy it must be quite a trial for you. I never was very fond of being led about on a string, I'm afraid.''

''Ain't many could do that,'' Reginald observed. He considered his cards for a moment before adding in a thoughtful voice, ''Though it appeared to me Miss Lindsay was able to return as good as you gave. Attractive creature, too—though of course she can't hold a candle to Miss Merivale as far as looks are concerned.'' He carelessly discarded an ace by mistake. ''Besides, her ladyship let slip that the poor girl's been left pretty much in the basket. Pity. Still, intriguing chit nonetheless, don't you agree?''

''You're asking a lot of questions tonight, Reggie,'' Giles noted dryly as he won the hand. ''I don't mean to throw a damper on your speculations, dear fellow, but let me assure you that my regard for the lady is of the most commonplace variety. We share an interest in art.''

''Truth?'' Reginald exclaimed in surprise. ''But how the devil—?'' He broke off, deterred by the forbidding expression on Giles's face. ''Now, Giles, no need to get upon your high ropes,'' he said quickly. ''Just curious. Talk about something else if you like. Let's forget Miss Lindsay altogether—and Miss Merivale, too, for that matter. Concentrate on the game instead, shall we?''

CURIOUSLY ENOUGH, the unsuspecting Fanny Merivale was the topic of a second conversation when the following morning Lady Hollinwood announced her intention of calling on the Merivales. While Athena accepted her invitation to bear her company, inwardly she was somewhat reluctant to further her acquaintance with the Beauty.

The two visitors were greeted enthusiastically upon their arrival in Hanover Square by Lady Merivale, a florid blonde with a taste in dress only a trifle more subdued than her friend's. She was widely acknowledged to be fiercely protective of her simple but doting husband and equally ambitious for her beautiful elder daughter. However, because she never made the least pretense of being anything else, she was generally forgiven for the first offense and more often than not commended for the second.

Since she and Lady Hollinwood at once embarked on a spirited dissection of the party, Athena was obliged to turn toward the young lady seated beside her on the opulent sofa.

Closer inspection revealed that Fanny Merivale's beauty lived up to its extravagant reputation. She presented a striking picture in a full-skirted robe trimmed with fluted muslin in a clear China blue that exactly matched her eyes and set off to a nicety her flawless complexion and shining blond curls. Nor could she be faulted for a lack of composure or address. Calmly setting aside the tambour frame on which she'd been working an uninspired floral embroidery, she inquired dutifully, "I collect you've but lately arrived in town, Miss Lindsay."

"Yes," Athena replied, matching her sedateness. "My father recently passed away, so we've come to stay with my aunt for a while." Then, bored with bland propriety, she leaned closer to create a properly confidential atmosphere and experimented with "There was a gentleman involved, you see. But then, I daresay you know how it is—" Athena sat back to observe the effect of her bait.

"Oh, yes," Fanny agreed, clearly reassessing her guest. "It's so very distasteful—is it not?—to find oneself the object of unwanted attentions," she added in the tone of a woman well versed in such matters. "However, I'll soon be beyond all of that. You see, I expect to be married very shortly." She lowered her eyes modestly.

"How delightful!" Athena cried, trying for a tone of girlish envy. "And the gentleman?"

"I rather think I shouldn't say just yet. While there's a firm understanding between us, I fancy Gile—that is, he wouldn't wish our attachment to be known before the marriage settlement has been arranged," Fanny concluded, making sure that the identity of the gentleman was perfectly clear.

Her artlessness seemed so precisely calculated that Athena was beginning to wonder whether Miss Merivale was truly the moonling she'd imagined her to be when a commotion at the door attracted everyone's attention.

"But indeed, I wasn't aware you had visitors, Mama," the cause of the hubbub protested after Lady Merivale had introduced her younger daughter, Sybil. "I only wished to ask Fanny if she'd be so kind as to help me set my cartoon to rights," she explained, holding up the sketch for a needlepoint and examining it with dissatisfaction.

"Well, it does look odd at that," Fanny allowed. "If you'd only chosen a simple design like my flowers, it wouldn't have mattered if the thing didn't turn out just so. Anyway, I'm sure I haven't the least idea how to change it now."

Concealing her eagerness, Athena leaned over to inspect the drawing. "If I may—?" she offered politely after a moment. "I collect you've got the perspective twisted around. The tree is farther away than the house, is it not? So it should be smaller, you see."

"Oh, thank you!" Sybil exclaimed happily. "But however did you learn about such things?"

Choosing her words carefully, Athena said, "Well, I had to work very hard. But then I was fortunate enough to have my father close by to teach me. Anyone who honestly wishes to improve must submit to instruction. Perhaps you've heard what Ben Johnson wrote in that regard: 'Art hath an enemy called Ignorance.' So, you see—"

"I see that you appear to be most admirably well schooled," Fanny put in. "However, I'm quite certain my artistic abilities were never called upon during my come-out. And I fail to see what use such a skill would be to me in running a household or entertaining guests." She preened a bit at the thought of how soon those tasks might occupy her days. "Indeed, Sybil, you'll spend your time far better, for instance, in practicing your quadrille figures, since dancing creditably is an accomplishment one may employ to good purpose both before and after a wedding." Fanny tucked her feet nicely beneath her and folded her hands in her lap with a self-satisfied air.

In all truthfulness, Athena was forced to acknowledge that there was little to dispute in Fanny's statements—provided that matrimony was indeed one's main object. She would have to discover a different approach, and soon, or be obliged to abandon her notion of being an instructress, she thought glumly as she rose to make her goodbyes and accompany her aunt to the door. And she very much wished she knew those other ways to achieve her goal, with which Giles Wescott had so recently tantalized her.

"MR. GILES WESCOTT, m'lady," the butler announced several hours later, much to the surprise of two of the ladies at the tea table.

If it wasn't enough that she'd forgotten to tell her aunt that he might call, Athena realized with a sinking feeling, the frankly calculating look that Lady Hollinwood shot in her direction warned her that her aunt intended to make much of the event.

No sooner had Giles entered the room than Lady Hollinwood exclaimed archly, "But surely this is a most unexpected pleasure, Wescott, to be honored by a second visit so close upon the first."

"The pleasure is entirely mine," Giles said smoothly, turning a droll face toward Athena. "I see you are up with the latest fashion," he said, having observed the copy of *Frankenstein* lying in Mrs. Lindsay's lap. "A furious controversy is raging, you know, over the identity of the author. Some claim it must be Byron and no one else, though I for one don't credit that for a moment. Still it's a splendid story. My mother sent me a copy directly upon publication, since we share an illicit taste for novels."

Lady Hollinwood stirred restively, and Giles soothed her by coming to the point. "I wondered, perhaps, if Miss Lindsay might care to venture out for a drive this afternoon?"

Faced with the enticing prospect of this sympathetic listener's company, Athena hesitated only briefly before agreeing. "Yes, I collect you offered to show me Carlton House," she invented for her aunt's sake. "If I may tear our guest away from such a learned discussion—?"

A few minutes later, as she was being handed once again into the stylish tilbury, she couldn't refrain from asking casually, "Have you truly read that book?"

"Yes, of course," Giles said in surprise. "I wouldn't fib about such a trifle. I believe an artist should be interested in other things besides art."

"But you are not an artist," Athena protested.

"No, though I once thought I would be," he said reflectively, suddenly stopping to throw an accusing look at her. "What the devil—? Do you know, you have the most unfortunate knack, Miss Lindsay, of making me confess the damnedest things.''

Athena laughed. "I expect it must be on account of my own wretched tongue, which will say what it shouldn't despite my very best efforts to prevent it. But pray continue, sir. After all,'' she pointed out, "you have my secret, so it's only fair that I should know yours.''

"Oh, very well," Giles conceded, "though I trust it's not much of a secret any longer. In my salad days I fancied myself something of a painter—that is to say, a natural artist, who had of course no need whatsoever of any instruction. So you may understand that it came as a shock when I discovered not only that my paintings did not take but that the universal opinion was that I lacked extraordinary talent, let us say. My family, I should tell you, were vastly relieved by this disclosure, and even happier when I outgrew this whim-wham and resumed my proper place in the world.''

"Why, I shouldn't have thought a man would be as subject to the dictates of society as a woman," Athena exclaimed.

"Dear me, but you're very severe," Giles said with a reproving frown. He halted the carriage to make way for a sedan chair carried by four hefty bearers. "Perhaps you might listen without passing any judgment.''

Athena sank back, abashed by her own lack of tact, and Giles slapped the reins and went on. "Once I'd determined that I wouldn't, after all, become an artist, I cast about for some means by which I might remain connected to that world. So, being blessed with an embarrassingly large fortune, I determined to become a collector and patron. The fact that I choose to waste the rhino in such a manner is acceptable, since spending an immoderate amount of cash is clearly something a gentleman may do without reproach, while having a profession is something he may not," he concluded in a rather bitter tone. "But to be fair, I should add that I've often wondered if it was the poor opinion of my family that made me put aside my drawing as much as the fear that I might actually fail."

This confession produced a companionable silence between them, which continued as they entered the park without either apparently feeling the need to resume the conversation.

Giles, however, was as little used to encountering silence from the young ladies he squired as he was to conducting such a serious discussion with them. That being the case, he felt obliged to direct Athena's attention to the passersby, pointing out the duke of York and Lord Harrowby as two of the prince regent's cronies, and then discoursing knowledgeably about such others as the duchess of Rutland and Lady Sefton. But she responded in such a disinterested fashion that he was finally moved to say, "Pray, don't stand on ceremony with me, Miss Lindsay. If there's something amiss, perhaps I may be of assistance."

Athena weighed her words carefully for a moment before admitting, "Not amiss, precisely, only a rather worrisome occurrence that's lately made me think.

Doesn't it seem to you, sir, that there's a contradiction between what is expected of us by others and what we may, in fact, do?'' She paused to determine whether Giles appeared to be following her reasoning, and concluding from his expression that he was, she continued more warmly. ''For example, before a certain age, young ladies are encouraged to acquire a proficiency in certain accomplishments in order—shall we say?—to enhance their attractiveness to the opposite sex. And yet once their object has been attained, every miss is just as promptly exhorted to put aside those same accomplishments without a backward glance or risk censure if she does not.''

''I take it that you believe the wedded state to be rather confining,'' Giles probed, halting the carriage again so as to devote his full attention to the discussion.

''Yes. But you know very well that it needn't be,'' Athena argued, ''for once she's married, a woman's position is secure, and for the most part she may do exactly what she likes. And yet I find it incomprehensible that most women make use of this new freedom only to engage in frivolity. Now, I ask you, sir—'' she turned up her hands in an earnest appeal ''—wouldn't you think it astonishing to discover that the woman you'd wed, who once could converse amusingly on any number of topics and perhaps also play the pianoforte and draw a little, was suddenly and wholly given over to buying clothes and jewelry and attending parties and such?''

"Indeed," Giles said. "Though I must say I scarcely think myself in danger of landing in that fix."

Athena looked to see if he was quizzing her, but his expression remained one of steadfast interest. "I daresay I shouldn't be speaking to you of such things," she said slowly, coloring up a bit, "only by your own admission I thought you might understand my predicament, and I, and I—"

"Have no one else with whom you may discuss such matters?" Giles supplied. "I collect her ladyship and Mrs. Lindsay are not precisely in your confidence. Though as yet, I should add, neither am I."

"Oh!" Athena exclaimed, blushing vividly. Suddenly aware that in her fervor she had moved closer to him than she had realized, she inched away. "How very stupid of me. Well, you see, it's only this: I thought that by coming to London—and Mama at first agreed—I'd be able to discover some young ladies in need of instruction in art and might succeed in establishing myself as a painting teacher. Our finances, you see, are rather at a pass. What's more, I hoped I might also discover some way of furthering my own painting and perhaps, as you know, even of securing a small commission or two. I trust I needn't tell you that neither of my relatives is aware of this second object, nor, I imagine, would they be inclined to approve of it if they were."

"No, I should think not. And do I apprehend, then, that you're finding the course a trifle rocky?" He sent Athena a sympathetic look.

"Yes," she confessed, searching his face for a moment, "for while I've located one or two possible students, I confess I haven't the least notion how to present myself for consideration as an instructress."

"Yes, I can see that might pose a problem. Especially since such a thing isn't commonly thought of as something that ladies do."

"Precisely what I was referring to earlier!" Athena exclaimed triumphantly. "And I must say that I can't fathom why it should be so."

"Nor I," Giles agreed. "And how—aside from our exchange at Ackermann's—are you faring in the second instance, if I may ask?"

"Oh, decidedly better," she assured him, her eyes beginning to twinkle. "Just the other day, in fact, Major Stebbing was wondering if I might be induced to make a sketch of his new bay."

"Of his horse? But then I should have guessed. Still, I can't believe that that elementary task would keep you occupied for long," he said, offering her a conspiratorial smile. "On account of your extensive experience with cows, you know."

This remark sent them off into peals of laughter, so that they were not immediately aware that another carriage had drawn up beside theirs and its two passengers were staring at them with considerable interest.

"Good afternoon," Fanny Merivale observed brightly, directing on them the full force of her smile. "I was only just saying to Hugh—are you acquainted with Lord Wetherford, Miss Lindsay?—that surely everything in town must be of the greatest curiosity to you, as you've only so very recently come up from Kent. In such a circumstance I'm sure anyone would find your remarks to be amusing. It must be quite refreshing to listen to someone whose conversation is practically guaranteed to be as simple and unaffected as yours.''

"Good afternoon, Fanny. Wetherford,'' Giles said heavily. "Well,'' he went on more energetically, "must be off! Don't want the horses to catch a chill.''

But before he could drive on, Fanny leaned over to lay a restraining hand on his arm. Looking intimately into his face, she fluttered her lashes and exclaimed throatily, "Heartless man! You haven't yet answered my note, and I did so hope I might count on you for tomorrow evening.'' Not waiting for a reply, she explained to Athena, "An invitation of long standing, Miss Lindsay. Merely a small theater party. But then,'' she added dubiously, "I daresay one addition to the party wouldn't matter a great deal—?''

"How very gracious of you to ask,'' Athena said coolly. "However, I fear my aunt already has plans for us.''

"What a pity,'' Fanny said perfunctorily. "But you won't disappoint me, will you?'' she coaxed prettily, training her lashes on Giles again.

"Probably not.'' With that noncommittal reply, Fanny appeared to be satisfied, for releasing her hold on his arm and favoring him with another brilliant smile, she at last allowed him to move the horses off at a brisk pace.

The return to Grosvenor Square was accomplished in a silence rather different from the peaceful sort of the outward journey. Finally, as Lady Hollinwood's house came into view, Giles ventured to say apologetically, "I hope you won't pay Miss Merivale any great mind, Miss Lindsay. She's sadly spoiled and altogether used to having her own way."

And most dangerous when thwarted, Athena thought to herself. "Oh, nonsense," she said lightly. "I assure you she doesn't discomfit me in the least."

"Excellent!" Giles replied with relief, remembering at the last minute to hand over Athena's drawings as he helped her down from the carriage. "May I call on you again at the end of the week? We need a few days to put the gossips off the trail. Though I promise I'll think about your problem in the meantime."

"If you wish," Athena said with a confusing mixture of relief and reluctance. "Your suggestions would be most welcome. But I expect," she added, as if to convince herself, "I'll be able to contrive a solution even without your assistance."

PRECISELY WHAT SORT of assistance he would be able to offer Athena wasn't turning out to be as easy to predict as he'd originally thought, Giles had to admit the following evening. Mindful of his promise and confident that his connections would ease her entry into artistic circles, he'd spent the afternoon in interviews with three distinguished leaders of the art fraternity with a notable lack of success.

Not, he realized, looking around at the group assembled at the Merivale residence, that anyone else would be the least interested in his endeavors, save, perhaps, for Reggie, on account of his friendship, and Miss Merivale herself, on account of her expectations.

Despite his distraction, however, Giles had to admire the cool calculation with which Fanny assigned her guests to the various carriages and disposed herself in his own. But the proprietary air she assumed toward him and the possessive way in which she'd hung on his arm from the moment he entered her house set his hackles up.

Disengaging himself with alacrity once they were seated in his coach, he advised her coldly, "I believe we'd do well to guard our conduct a little more closely, Miss Merivale, or we'll soon have everyone believing there's some secret attachment between us."

Fanny had the grace to blush. However, never one to hesitate in turning a situation to advantage, she lowered her lashes, and looking through them in the fashion of a practiced flirt, she inquired in honeyed tones, "And should you dislike that so very much, sir?"

"Not," he assured her bluntly, "if it were true." He paused for a moment to study Fanny's beautiful face more carefully and then asked with an apparent lack of interest, "And should you?"

"I collect that's not precisely an offer," Fanny said calmly, not the least discomfited by such a brusque question. "Very well, then. Since you obviously wish us to speak plainly with each other, I will tell you that I believe I'd quite enjoy being married to you."

"Indeed?" Giles said in an undefinable tone. "And yet I'd no notion that your sentiments were thus engaged."

"But surely there isn't the slightest necessity for that," Fanny replied composedly. She added quickly after a glance at his expression, "Of course, I'll like very well being your wife and mistress of your households. And owing to our respective positions, you must admit it's fully expected that we'll make a match."

"I see," Giles said politely. "This is to be, I take it, a marriage of convenience, then."

"Why, naturally!" Fanny exclaimed in surprise. "Such an alliance is, after all, entirely suitable for members of our set, is it not? To be sure, I do feel a certain affection for you. However, I'm not so green as to require that ours should be a love match. I shouldn't wish at all to be like those ill-guided women who lower themselves by exhibiting an immodest jealousy of their husbands' time or his companions. And am I right that you, sir, wouldn't encourage a wife to act in such an unbecoming manner? No, indeed," she informed him without waiting for a reply. "Of course, I'll be entirely agreeable to fulfilling all my marital obligations." She paused to stare out the window at the crowded street for a suitably meaningful moment. "Nevertheless, I expect that in private we'll continue to lead our separate lives—in a circumspect fashion, of course."

"Should you?" Giles said thoughtfully as he tapped his knee with a clenched hand. "And I take it, then, that you wouldn't accompany me when I go abroad to collect paintings."

"Definitely not," Fanny replied firmly. "I haven't the least desire to be dragged about for weeks on end from one questionable inn to another, surrounded all the while by strangers—and foreigners at that." She bent down to fluff the net frock covering her blue satin slip and assure herself that the blond lace hem was not being crushed. "Such things I'll be happy to leave in your more experienced hands," she said winningly before spoiling the effect by adding, "And besides, I've no great interest in the arts. My own tastes run rather more to the entertainments of town life."

And to frivolous amusements such as parties and gowns, Giles thought, mindful of a recent conversation on the subject. In light of that exchange with Athena Lindsay, the divine Fanny didn't acquit herself very well. Her extraordinary beauty and the admirable ease with which she moved through every social situation were above reproach. Even so, he couldn't deny that more often than not he found her conversation limited, her interests narrow and her behavior decidedly self-indulgent. But more distressing was the cool and unemotional manner in which she'd entered into the discussion about her future. Although he, too, had been taught that a loveless marriage might not be outside the realm of possibility, he was still enough of a romantic to hope for a love union. And the prospect of allying himself with a woman who approached the matter as if she were ordering a new dress was so dismal that he lapsed into a troubled silence.

His thoughts were interrupted as they neared the theater when Fanny said complacently, as if the answer were a foregone conclusion, "Shall I tell my father, then, that you'll wait upon him tomorrow, sir?"

Now, whether it was because of the previous afternoon's encounter in the park and his consequent reassessment of the two women or because he felt that he was being pushed into taking an irrevocable step, Giles couldn't later have stated with certainty. For the moment, he was conscious only of an overwhelming desire to dash the satisfied expression from his companion's face. Therefore, he answered without pausing to consider the consequences, "You may tell him whatever you like. What I shall do, though, is another matter entirely."

The furious look Fanny directed at him before flouncing out of the carriage was not, he reflected, so very different from the one he recalled seeing on the face of a man who, having loudly proclaimed himself a splendid shot, had let fly at a pheasant, only to bag a crow instead.

Buoyed up by this reminiscence, he strolled calmly into the Theatre Royal after his hostess. When Fanny seated herself ostentatiously beside Lord Wetherford, Giles quietly took a place in the rear of the box.

Naturally, this arrangement didn't escape the notice of the rest of the guests, and Reginald at once leaned over to hiss accusingly, "Been throwing your tongue about, Giles?"

Happily for their friendship, however, Giles was spared the necessity of a reply, for just then the lights dimmed, the curtain ascended, and the performance began.

GILES WAS RATHER SURPRISED to discover that Reginald continued to take the task of calling him to order quite seriously. They had scarcely left 13 Bond Street, where Giles had donned the gloves to go his weekly five rounds with Gentleman John Jackson, to stroll home when he found himself being relentlessly questioned about his interest in the young lady on whose behalf he'd occupied himself the past several days.

"The thing is, my boy," Reginald was saying with an elaborately nonchalant air, "I thought it was just a hum myself at first. Kind of escapade you're famous for. But really, Giles, running all over town applying to one and all to give a leg up to an artist no one's ever heard of, and a mere chit of a girl at that. No, no, dear fellow, it won't do by half." He shook his head sorrowfully, perhaps at the Pomona-green waistcoat overlaid by rivulets of indigo displayed in a nearby shop window.

"I'd just as soon you steered clear of my affairs, Reggie, as I believe I've often asked you to do in the past." Giles examined his knuckles for bruises, flexing his hands in what his friend felt to be a most alarming manner, given his recent exhibition with the famous boxer.

"Like to," Reginald said in all sincerity. "But the trouble is, when someone as full of juice as you are begins to make a cake of himself over a female, it ain't long before some forty-jawed person will seek to do him a mischief. Well, couldn't allow that to happen."

By this time they had arrived at Piccadilly and were nerving themselves to plunge through the streams of carts and carriages, coaches and horsemen, to the other side.

"Reggie, my dear fellow, you positively unman me by your constant devotion to my well-being," Giles said sarcastically.

"Always happy to be of service," Reginald called modestly over his shoulder as he dodged an enormous brewer's dray pulled by four massive horses.

He took up the thread again when Giles had rejoined him and they were turning into St. James's Street. "Rather enjoy the way you've managed to diddle the dupes, I must say. Still, you must have known I'd be able to smell out a hoax when I found one. Well, I mean it's been all over town for several days now that Wetherford and Miss Merivale have reached an understanding, and yet you haven't even offered up two words about it. Stands to reason, then, that there must be someone else who's caught your fancy. And at any rate, your solicitude for a certain lady don't exactly support the pretext that it's all on account of a shared interest in art."

"I don't suppose, Reggie, that you might be induced to credit my lack of response to the fact that I've discovered I don't care a jot for what Miss Merivale does or doesn't do."

"Not," Reginald assured him, "when coupled with the three-piled compliments you heap upon the other young lady at every opportunity."

"Just because I've chosen to make known to you my appreciation for some of Miss Lindsay's finer qualities don't mean I'm readying to post the banns," Giles complained peevishly. "She might become a deuced good painter if given half a chance, but dash it if I can find a way to be of assistance to her in the whole cursed thing, despite my promise that I should."

There being no possible response to this comment, a short silence followed, during which both gentlemen watched a smart young footman trying to snatch a kiss from a bridling maid.

Finally, his brow furrowed from the effort of articulating his thoughts, Reginald said slowly, "Believe I've heard that Beaumont fellow droning on about how ofttimes he lets artists come to his house. Says all they want is just to sit and stare and sketch away for hours on end, learning to make copies of what he calls the old masters. Well, the thing is, Giles, since your collection is said to go Beaumont's one better, it occurs to me you might invite Miss Lindsay to do as he would."

Giles stepped back to regard him in admiration. "I never imagined you could be so very inventive, Reggie." He took Reginald's arm and propelled him forward. "I conceived of that notion too, but have concluded that it simply won't wash. Even if I did make such an offer to the lady, what then? In the first place, she'd need someone to tell her if she'd done the copies right, and then what would she do with the damned things afterwards? She couldn't sell them off except as copies, and where would that get her? No," he finished sadly with a shake of his head, "I'm afraid she wouldn't make very tolerable progress if we followed that course. No..."

Giles slowed his steps and gazed unseeing down the street. Reginald followed suit.

"What's required is some way for her to secure a patron and thence a commission.... Of course—" Giles picked up speed again "—I could always offer her a commission myself." He started to brighten at the idea. Then he shrugged. "But since I haven't been always on the right-about with her, she might wonder at my motives and even deny herself special treatment at my hands. Because of my past conduct, you see, I doubt she'd believe I could do business with her in a strictly disinterested fashion," he concluded, looking crestfallen once again.

Reginald, who had been schooled in the niceties of polite conversation, refrained with some difficulty from begging for the particulars. He was just on the point of weakening when Giles was struck by a sudden inspiration.

Whipping around like a hare flushed from cover, Giles stared him full in the face and exclaimed, "You can do it, Reggie!"

"Well, I daresay I can..." he ventured in some confusion.

"Of course you can," Giles declared impatiently. "You," he explained, looking inordinately pleased with the idea, "shall offer Miss Lindsay the commission."

Reginald was taken aback. "I?" he said in amazement, sagging for a moment against a handy Corinthian column guarding an imposing housefront. "Glad to be of assistance, dear boy, but I haven't the least taste for such things, you know."

"Not for yourself, you widgeon, for me!" Giles exclaimed as he tugged him along. "No one would ever suspect you of plotting a mischief. And surely," he said in a more cajoling manner, "you see that you're the very person to convince the lady of the sincerity of my—that is to say, of your intentions."

Tactfully freeing his sleeve from his friend's grasp, Reginald swelled with pride at this praise.

"Now, then, what shall we say is the occasion for which the painting is to be ordered?"

"Gift for my parents?" Reginald volunteered, settling his coat again to his satisfaction. "Come as a bit of a surprise to them, of course. Fancy the last token of my esteem was a mongrel pup I presented to my mother when I was about ten. Didn't like it, either, as I recall, because the silly pup would smear mud all over her gown every time he saw her and she never could get it to come clean—" He broke off, having observed the exasperated look on his friend's face.

"Beg pardon, Giles," he said penitently. "Keep forgetting the thing's meant to be for you."

"Evidently," Giles muttered. He considered his friend's suggestion. "No, I don't believe that will fadge," he admitted at last. "Your parents are due to arrive in town shortly, are they not? What if Miss Lindsay should be introduced to them and inquire innocently enough about the painting?"

Much to his own astonishment, Reginald succeeded in producing an acceptable idea. "Why not tell her," he offered helpfully, "that it's to be a surprise?"

"I expect that's precisely what we should say," Giles agreed. "Besides, I don't imagine we ought to embroil anyone else in this little scheme. Be bad enough if it's discovered and the two of us end up looking like jackpuddings." Noting that this ill-chosen remark had tempered Reginald's confidence, he added reassuringly, "However, there's not the least need, I promise you, to consider that eventuality—provided that we keep our wits about us."

A second silence ensued. Finally, Reginald, who had passed the time first in searching the street for some means of deliverance and then in wondering vainly how his friend might be persuaded to give up the entire notion, was startled out of his reverie by a shout.

"Why, that's the ticket!" Giles exclaimed triumphantly to the surprise of one respectable elderly lady and two dirty little boys. "We'll say it's to be a present for your betrothed!"

"My what?" Reginald inquired faintly, looking quickly around to see if they were overheard. "But surely you can't have forgotten that I ain't in the petticoat line?"

"Of course not," Giles replied scornfully. "We'll only pretend that you are. And secretly betrothed, too, I think, so that we may extract a vow of silence from Miss Lindsay. Yes, I warrant such a secret betrothal will suit our purposes admirably."

"But Giles, do you really think—?"

"Most definitely," Giles assured him. He couldn't resist adding slyly, "Besides, who will suspect? And after all, my peacock, you must admit that you'd make an incomparable bridegroom."

Reginald could barely suppress a shudder at the dreadful vision this compliment evoked.

The two stopped at the corner of Pall Mall before separating to walk to their respective residences. But still not convinced of the advisability of entering into such a deception, Reginald felt called upon to point out, "Must say it appears it's you, dear boy, who'll be thought the scoundrel if Miss Lindsay deduces what we're about."

"Stuff!" Giles exclaimed cheerfully. "I've already told you—there ain't the least possibility of that."

CHAPTER FIVE

THE FOLLOWING MORNING, Athena decided to act on her decision to call at the Stebbing's London residence, for she was curious to discover whether Elizabeth Stebbing might not, with a little encouragement, prove a lasting friend and ally. Long ago she had given up hoping to light on even one of her contemporaries who was genuinely interested in any of the arts and who felt self-improvement as worthwhile as philanthropic efforts to improve other people. But now she was tempted to believe that Elizabeth's musical abilities marked her out as a lady with serious aspirations—and so perhaps as one who might prove sympathetic to Athena's own ambitions.

Upon being shown into a private sitting room, however, Athena was surprised to discover a scene distinctly at odds with what she had thought Elizabeth's character to be. Books lay piled in dangerously high stacks on the floor and furniture, and music sheets were strewn haphazardly here and there. In the midst of this confusion sat Elizabeth, resolutely sewing a torn shawl. Observing the comical expression on her visitor's face, she smiled shyly.

"Welcome to my lair, Miss Lindsay," she said. "I imagine you must have been expecting something a trifle more restrained."

"I must confess I find this to be a most delightful contrast to the apartments at my aunt's house," Athena replied, adding conscientiously, "Though I assure you she perfectly provides me with all that I could want."

"Indeed, I do hope you find this comfortable," Elizabeth said, gazing somewhat dubiously around the room. "I must tell you that Papa—who was used to a military life and who even now spends only as little time indoors as he absolutely has to—isn't terribly sensitive to the amenities that others take as a matter of course. However," she confided, losing a little of her reserve, "I find the compensations to be many, since I'm never obliged to attend much to housekeeping and may instead apportion my time quite as I like."

"How very glad I should be if I were able to do likewise!" Athena exclaimed enviously, moving aside three books and a pair of slippers and seating herself companionably on a couch. "When my father was alive, I was obliged to discharge most of the domestic tasks, since poor Mama has little talent and even less interest in housekeeping. And even though we now reside with my aunt, I must say the situation hasn't greatly improved. In fact, Aunt Louisa is forever discovering yet another errand I must execute immediately. What's more, she is not, I should tell you, in the least sympathetic to my love for art. Sometimes I can very nearly believe that her requests are a deliberate attempt to keep me busy anywhere but at my drawing."

"Then I'm indeed fortunate," Elizabeth admitted slowly, "for Miss Palmer is perfectly in sympathy with my aims and often shields me from the tasks she knows I like the least. I truly can't imagine how I'd contrive half as well without her assistance. My mother died, you see, before I was out of the nursery, and Lucy has been my governess—my companion, really—since then. In fact, I'd count myself entirely happy if I were simply allowed to continue just as I have, with my books and my music and dear Lucy for company." A small sigh escaped her. "That was all very well once, but now that I'm past eighteen, I fancy Papa hasn't the slightest notion what to do with me any longer. I made my come-out last season, and I fear—I fear I didn't take. All that enormous bother, and yet poor Papa still hasn't received a single offer for my hand." She blushed vividly and stammered, "I daresay you don't understand."

"Oh, but I do," Athena said feelingly, offering Elizabeth a sympathetic smile. "Indeed, I quite comprehend your situation. But tell me—do you even wish to be married?"

"Not if—I mean— Well, perhaps if David—that is, Mr. Holt— Though truly, I can't become used to calling him mister because we played together practically every day when we were little. Of course," she added with a wistful air, "now that we're in town, we don't have much occasion to see each other any more."

"Do I take it that you feel a certain tenderness for this Mr. Holt?" Athena inquired tactfully.

"Well, he is quite devoted to me," Elizabeth admitted, laying aside her mending, which by now she had crumpled into a small ball. "And at one time I think we both just expected that we'd form a lasting attachment. We've been friends since we were in the nursery, and we're neighbors, as well. But then Papa decided it would be more broadening if we were to reside in town. I do believe he honestly wants what is best for me and not, as Lucy insists, that he merely hopes to find a better match. Still," she continued unevenly, clasping and reclasping her hands, "it does seem as if I'm always having to choose between situations that might be beneficial and those I know to be easy and comfortable and so a good deal more pleasant. And Mr. Holt is a very comfortable sort of person...."

"I see," Athena murmured. "I imagine you've had a fairly difficult time of it, then."

"Yes," Elizabeth admitted in an unself-conscious way that quite disarmed her listener. "You see, Papa has done so much for me that I think it altogether my duty to accede to whatever he wishes me to do. But on account of having been in the army, he is very strict, and although dear Lucy often speaks for me, she's a trifle afraid of him. I'm not afraid of him precisely, but you saw yourself that he treats me like a child." She stared earnestly at Athena for a moment before dropping her eyes to her hands. "Ordinarily, I don't mind too much if that is what people think, but I should so very much like you to think otherwise."

"Oh, but I do," Athena assured her. She rose and crossed the room to nestle cozily on the footstool beside Elizabeth's chair. "And as far as others are concerned, you need only resolve to forgo the dubious pleasure of knowing that everyone holds a good opinion of you. After all, the world already believes that artists are an eccentric lot—and I, for one, don't care a whit what others think of me," she declared blithely, recent examples to the contrary notwithstanding.

"Yes, I can see that such an attitude would serve very well for you," Elizabeth agreed with an admiring smile. "But I confess I don't think myself capable of living outside the bounds of society. Shouldn't you be lonely?"

"Oh, but I'm not suggesting doing this alone," Athena said comfortingly. "It's altogether essential to have at least one close friend who is truly sympathetic and trustworthy—don't you agree, Elizabeth? I may call you Elizabeth, may I not? After all, I've already promised your father we are to be in each other's pockets, so we may as well dispense with the formalities now."

"I quite agree!" Elizabeth exclaimed happily.

DESPITE WHAT SHE'D TOLD Elizabeth, however, Athena was conscious of feeling a trifle lonely as she made her way slowly back along Oxford Street in the direction of Grosvenor Square. In fact, over the last several days she'd gradually become aware of the number of occasions on which she'd longed to discuss her impressions with a certain gentleman she knew would have shared the humor of each situation.

That she had expected Mr. Wescott to call again by now wasn't altogether surprising, given his promise to suggest ways of advancing her career as an artist. But that she should find herself actively missing his company as well as his conversation was a good deal more unsettling, Athena concluded, climbing the steps to her aunt's house.

It was too much to expect, however, that her ladyship might allow her niece to retire to her room undisturbed after her outing. Scarcely had Athena begun to take off her gloves when a peremptory knock on the door was immediately followed by the entrance of her aunt.

Athena wasn't so completely abstracted that she failed to notice the elaborate casualness with which Lady Hollinwood mentioned that Reginald Thurston had come to call while she was out.

"And most insistent he was, too," her ladyship said. She settled her well-rounded form on an elegant Grecian-style couch near the windows. "He was dressed in his best bib and tucker, of course. Informed me his neckcloth was tied in some ridiculousness called the horse collar. Well, and it did look like one at that, because if the poor fellow could turn his head so much as a whisker, then you may call me a duchess."

At this point, Athena, well aware that her aunt could continue forever in this vein quite happily, interrupted. "And did you two discuss anything else of note?" she inquired in what she trusted was a circumspect fashion as she removed her bonnet and shook out her curls.

Lady Hollinwood shot her niece one of her penetrating looks. "Upon my world, child, you must think me a green one. I can see how matters stand. Why, it's plain as a pikestaff! But—" she wagged a warning finger "—mind you don't come to grief, now, playing one off against the other. I must say it's my experience that if a man is forced to choose between a woman and his best friend, he'll pick the friend every time."

Athena was somewhat at a loss. Since she'd scarcely exchanged three words with Reginald Thurston on the one evening on which they had met, she couldn't help feeling it was a little fanciful of her aunt to attribute any deep significance to that event, let alone an intention to encourage him to vie with Giles Wescott for her favors. And particularly, she thought, slipping out of her pelisse, when it was quite obvious that although Mr. Thurston might enjoy the admiration of the fair sex, he would certainly elect to pass his time in the company of his own. If she was privately inclined to think that he might have come bearing a message from another party, she saw no need to point this out to her aunt. However, that possibility promptly made her blush in a way that could only confirm her relative's suspicions. Deciding to take advantage of that fact, she lowered her eyes and asked in a coy manner, "Perhaps he will return tomorrow?"

"I collect he did say something of the kind," her ladyship admitted grudgingly. "So you can be missish when you please," she said with evident satisfaction. "Well, and who's to say that that stratagem won't turn the trick? Of course, I've never known Thurston to be smitten before, but still, I fancy any relation of mine would make as eligible a partner as he might want," she declared complacently, and with that Parthian shot she hoisted herself up from her comfortable perch and at last sailed out of the room.

THE FOLLOWING AFTERNOON found the three ladies assembled in the sitting room, where Lady Hollinwood had undertaken to teach her sister-in-law how to play piquet. The success of this enterprise was soon threatened, however, when her ladyship began attempting to explain the game's intricate scoring system to Mrs. Lindsay. In fact, once she stated that a player with a hand containing only number cards could gain ten points by claiming *carte blanche*, any semblance of order was altogether lost as the three ladies immediately dissolved into laughter—unluckily Lady Hollinwood had explained over luncheon that the identical term was used when a gentleman proposed an intimate connection with a woman of a certain class.

It was into this raucous atmosphere that Reginald Thurston strolled a few minutes later on the heels of her ladyship's butler. He was so struck by the expressions on the three faces turned in his direction that he was moved to exclaim, "Convivial group you make, I assure you." He crossed the floor to bow before his hostess. "Trust there's little need to inquire if you're enjoying your visit, Miss Lindsay."

"Oh, perfectly," she assured him, dragging her eyes away from the emerald tiepin the size of a robin's egg that adorned his neckcloth. "Before I arrived in London, I'd no notion whatsoever that town life would prove so very enlightening."

Reginald, who was the first to admit that witticisms were not his strong suit, took this remark at face value. "Do you know, that's just what my father told me when I was preparing to come down from Oxford. 'Reggie,' he said, 'I've no doubt you'll find this a most enlightening experience.' And so, indeed, I have."

This anecdote put a damper on the conversation, and a short silence ensued. Athena at last undertook to remark pointedly on the lovely spring weather they'd been having.

Her effort was rewarded by a grateful smile. "Be delighted to take you for a drive round the park," Reginald proposed. "There's an uncommon lot of posies and such in bloom just now. No doubt you'd fancy seeing them. Most of the ladies seem to."

"Why, yes, I daresay I should," Athena agreed at once.

"I thought you were accustomed to go astride, Thurston," Lady Hollinwood said abruptly, loudly tamping the cards together on the edge of the table.

"Well, ofttimes I do," he confirmed. "The thing is, I've just been delivered a new turn-out from Win-

dus—designed to my own specifications, of course—
and I'm quite on tenterhooks till I find out how it
goes.''

Naturally it wasn't to be presumed that the newest
conveyance of a gentleman who claimed membership
in both the Whip and the Defiance as well as the Four-
in-Hand Club would be cut at all in the ordinary
mode. Though Athena had heard of a high-perch
phaeton, she still wasn't prepared to be confronted by
a vehicle with a tiny seat suspended a full foot above
her head. If that wasn't outstanding enough, the coach
itself was painted a glossy sapphire, the spokes of the
wheels picked out in citron and the whole of the inte-
rior covered with heavy gold silk.

Once they were under way, though, Athena found
her lofty vantage point so unexpectedly exhilarating
that she cried breathlessly that she felt quite as if she
were flying through the air.

This remark caused Reginald to cast a furtive glance
around as if he feared they were being pursued. In
fact, now that Athena thought about it, he had grown
increasingly ill at ease since the moment they'd left her
aunt's house. After another apprehensive look
around, he snapped the reins so vigorously that the
horses were fairly put along. Leaning toward her, Reginald yelled hoarsely in a disjointed voice made worse
by the violent swaying of the carriage, ''Wait till we
gain the park. Can't talk now—don't wish to be overheard. Got something important to discuss!''

Though her curiosity threatened to get the better of
her manners, Athena managed to resist broaching

even one of the many questions that sprang immediately to mind. She was aided by the hair-raising nature of the drive, which made conversation difficult if not downright impossible.

However, no sooner had they gained the boundary of the park and Reginald had pulled the horses back to a more sedate pace than she at once straightened her bonnet and demanded impatiently, "Well, sir? I collect you told me you've something of interest to impart."

"So I did," Reginald conceded, his eyes flicking nervously to left and right. He lowered his voice. "What I want to say is, it happens that I've become betrothed."

"Indeed?" Athena said, wrinkling her brow in confusion. "My felicitations, then, sir. And the lady, if I may inquire—?"

"No!" he blurted out. "It's a secret. That is, hasn't made her come-out yet," he invented rapidly. "A secret betrothal. Simple country miss. Quite unsophisticated—refreshingly so, actually. Known her for years. Cradle friends, you see," he confided, borrowing freely from the experience of one of those whom he termed his less fortunate friends.

"But that's all downriver of the matter about which I want to consult you," he continued in a more resolute tone. "The thing is, obliged to devise a gift to mark the occasion. Only proper, you know. But it appears the lady don't have a taste for gewgaws. Turns out she's got a deuced queer fancy for art instead." He forgot himself sufficiently to purse his lips at such an unfashionable inclination before hurrying on. "More to the point, Giles has told me—in strictest confidence, mind—that you're a prime hand at such things. Naturally it put me to wondering if you would be willing to do me the service of executing a painting to give to the lady," he concluded in a rush, clearly relieved to have gotten this speech behind him. "Pay the going tariff, of course. Giles said he thought seventy-five pounds would be in order."

"Delighted!" Athena agreed, thrusting aside practical considerations in favor of anticipating the enjoyment she would get from transferring his unique image to canvas. "Face only or full figure? I should think full-length would be best in order to capture the complete effect. But then, perhaps you'd prefer a miniature. They do tend to be favorites with the ladies. Still, I'd advise a larger rendering. Much more impressive in your case, I fancy," she declared in all sincerity, allowing her eyes to rove over the peculiarities of his costume.

"Oh, no—definitely not a portrait," Reginald protested, drawing back in horror as he vividly imagined Giles's reaction to being presented with a painting of his best friend and confidant.

Athena regarded him in surprise. "But I assure you, sir, a portrait would be entirely unexceptional."

"Precisely," he pointed out, with a stroke of inspiration that would have done credit to a cleverer man. "Too sadly common by half. I'd never wish to hear it claimed that I was ever a shade behindhand in the mode."

"But if not a portrait, what, then?" Athena asked, raising her eyebrows to direct a quizzical look at him.

This simple question threw Reginald into considerable turmoil. In point of fact, the scheme having been very hastily devised, neither he nor his fellow conspirator had even spared a thought for so elementary a matter as the subject of the proposed painting. Snapping the reins to bring the horses up to a trot, he indulged briefly in a tiny sigh and a vain wish that he might suddenly find himself anywhere but in the middle of Hyde Park embroiled in a game that now appeared to be slipping inexorably from his grasp.

"But you're the artist, after all," he said in a plaintive voice. "Mean to say you ain't got anything to suggest? I promise I'll be guided by whatever you propose."

"But didn't you tell me, sir, that you've been acquainted with the lady since your nursery days?" Athena persisted. She stared at him in a considering way, beginning to feel there was something about his story that failed to hold water. "Surely you must have some notion of what she'd be likely to enjoy," she pointed out with merciless logic.

"Oh, indeed," Reginald assured her, nodding vigorously while wondering how he could ascribe the preferences of the work's patron to some mythical member of the opposite sex. "But frankly, not the sort of thing I'd be bound to notice," he admitted in all honesty, now shaking his head from side to side and peering anxiously ahead as if on the lookout for something he fully expected to find along the route.

"Hallo!" he cried in happy surprise. "Here's Giles. Dashed clever fellow. Shouldn't wonder if he can't pull us out of this cursed muddle. What luck!"

Athena couldn't agree. At the sight of the approaching figure astride a handsome chestnut, she suddenly found herself preoccupied with a strange pounding in her chest and a curious inability to catch her breath.

How at home he looks on that horse, she thought, greedily absorbing every detail of the way his riding clothes were molded to his powerful physique and the confidence with which he managed the nervous chestnut that clearly didn't know what to make of a high-perch phaeton. *And how I'd love to paint him exactly like this,* she realized, observing how the sunlight had turned his hair a luminous bluish-black and browned the surprisingly delicate hand that held the reins so firmly.

"Afternoon Reggie, Miss Lindsay." Giles sketched a half bow and gave them both a warm smile. "How delighted I am to have encountered you today," he said, turning in his saddle to address Athena more directly. "Especially when everything hereabouts has been so deuced flat of late—eh, Reggie?"

"Why, no, Giles—wouldn't say that at all," his friend objected with a frown. "You can't have forgotten the latest gossip we heard about old Rotherby and that ladybird from the Haymarket. Or how we saw poor Gliddons tooling his coach through St. James's as if a pack of hounds were after him. Or—"

"I rather fancy," Giles interrupted in a steely drawl, "that it's you who've forgotten that a gentleman don't commonly refer to such events when in the company of a lady."

Reginald appeared properly dashed. "Beg pardon, I'm sure," he mumbled before adding, much to Athena's edification, "Still, it ain't greatly to be wondered at, Giles. You said yourself she wasn't cut out of ordinary cloth.

"Besides," he continued, failing entirely to observe his friend shifting uncomfortably on his mount at this incautious remark, "seeing you puts me in mind of what we were discussing when we met you. You know—the painting for my intended. The thingummy you suggested Miss Lindsay might agree to undertake on my behalf."

"Yes?" Giles said, his eyes darting quickly from one to the other. "Anything amiss?"

"Not precisely," Athena began. "Only—really, it's too foolish for words, but we can't seem to agree on a subject. You see, I suggested a portrait, which you must concede would be eminently suitable. However, Mr. Thurston thinks a portrait is too conventional."

"How very wise of him." Giles stared absently into the distance for a moment before advising, "Do you know, I shouldn't wonder if something a trifle more dramatic, shall we say, and somewhat grander in scope wouldn't come a good deal closer to satisfying the recipient's taste."

"Oh!" Athena exclaimed in surprise. "Are you acquainted with the lady, then?"

"Intimately," he assured her blandly. "We share an appreciation for art. And since, as you're doubtless aware, poor Reggie does not, she and I find that we're the most sympathetic of souls. It's hardly to be credited how very nearly our tastes coincide. Don't you agree, Reggie?"

Reginald immediately became very red in the face and cast a look of helpless supplication at Giles. Finding no help in that quarter, he managed to get out in a choked voice that such was indeed the case.

Faced with Reginald's embarrassment and blank ignorance of his wife-to-be and Giles's extraordinary familiarity with her taste, Athena had become at first bewildered and then skeptical. Ever since Giles had begun to speak, a suspicion had been growing steadily in her mind that it was actually he, not Reginald, who had secretly become betrothed. Why they should apparently have agreed to make her believe otherwise was puzzling indeed, she decided, looking first at the gentleman on the horse and then at the one in the carriage.

But in all honesty, she admitted silently, turning quite pale at the thought, the young lady's identity was far more important to her than anything else—given the recent proof that her interest in Giles, if not her affection, was already firmly engaged. Miss Merivale clearly couldn't be the one, since nothing stood in the way of an open announcement of betrothal to her and art was certainly not among her interests. But if not Miss Merivale, then who?

Athena fixed her eyes on a row of pink tulips, steadfastly ignoring the hard way Giles was staring at his friend and the difficult time Reginald was having not squirming under that scrutiny. However, it was clear that neither gentleman felt it necessary to offer any further information in order to secure her coop-eration. Since the prospect of making any inquiries herself made her feel decidedly uncomfortable and there was nothing to be gained from letting it be known that she'd guessed their secret, the issue was destined to remain unresolved for the present.

"In that case," she said at last in a formal manner, "perhaps you'd like me to submit a few sketches for both of you to examine."

Giles was surprised that Athena had suddenly be-come rather withdrawn and now spoke in a distant voice remarkably at odds with her former friendly manner. He told himself, however, that she'd prob-ably only fallen prey to the anxiety produced by what was, after all, her first legitimate commission. So with that conclusion firmly in mind, he smiled encourag-ingly at her. "There isn't the least need to put your-self in a taking over such a milk-and-water matter. I'm convinced we'll easily be able to arrive at some agree-ment once we've had time to review your ideas."

"Got a notion—fix on a date now," Reginald urged. "Save no end of bother," he pointed out ner-vously, wishful of concluding the business at hand as quickly as possible.

"Yes, why don't we say—?" Giles began.

"Oh, what a little goose I am not to have thought of it sooner!" Athena suddenly bobbed up in her seat and had to clutch the side of the carriage to avoid falling out. "Where am I to work? It can't be at my aunt's house, for she doesn't at all approve of this hobby of mine, as she puts it. And even if she did, I'd scarcely find an opportunity to paint, since I'm forever obliged to put aside my work in order to wait on her pleasure. We shall have to conceal the whole scheme from her." She regarded the two men in dismay.

"Can't use my quarters," Reginald protested without waiting to be asked. "Bachelor apartment. Wouldn't be fitting at all."

"No, nor mine," Giles said slowly. "But surely there must be someplace you might contrive to visit daily without arousing suspicion."

Athena brightened and shot him a grateful look. "Of course—Elizabeth Stebbing's. We've struck up a great friendship, you see, and I'm confident that she'll be happy to assist in whatever way she can. Though I'll have to tell her our secret, you know," she added apologetically. "But even so, there isn't any reason why that should prove worrisome, since she's the most trustworthy of individuals, I promise you."

Although Reginald at first was not persuaded they were wise to increase the number of those who knew of his impending nuptials, he was convinced in the end by the sheer strength of Giles's presence, if not by the force of his logic. Surely Reggie could see that without applying to Miss Stebbing for assistance, their enterprise was doomed at the outset. And naturally he didn't—did he?—wish that to occur. Uneasily agreeing at last in the face of a stern look from Giles and a beseeching look from Athena that he would not wish their enterprise to be doomed, Reginald listened fretfully as plans were accordingly laid.

Only after it had been settled that they would meet again on Monday afternoon next did the trio finally move to disperse, allowing Reginald to slap the reins with obvious relief and put an end to what he later described as one of the most taxing afternoons he'd ever endured.

If the other two were also aware of serious misgivings about the scheme, neither—unwisely perhaps—was prepared at this point to acknowledge them.

CHAPTER SIX

SINCE THE FOREMOST MATTER to be resolved was whether she could secure Elizabeth Stebbing's support for her artistic enterprise, Athena was understandably eager to pay her a visit. Accordingly, she lost little time the following morning in arranging to make a stop in Cavendish Square. And no sooner had she been directed into the private sitting room than she dropped into the nearest chair and offered up a recital of the previous afternoon's events. She decided at the last minute to omit any mention of her suspicions about the identity of the prospective bridegroom and to adhere instead only to what had actually transpired. But even so, her narrative was so unsystematic and her manner so unusually self-conscious that it was quite to Elizabeth's credit that neither of those circumstances discomposed her.

After putting to Athena one or two simple questions, Elizabeth turned to her governess, whom Athena had scarcely noticed until that point, and said thoughtfully, as if the matter were already an accomplished fact, "I think mornings would be best, don't you, Lucy?"

"Definitely, my dear," Miss Palmer said promptly. She rose from her chair in the corner and assumed the posture of a lecturer. She was a tall, spare woman of close on forty with a large, square face and brown hair already beginning to gray. She was wearing a plain dress, as befitted her calling and also her upbringing as one of six daughters of a country clergyman. But the obvious fondness with which she addressed her young charge reminded Athena of the special place she held in Elizabeth's heart.

"Sometime ago Beth and I discovered," Miss Palmer said, "that much can be accomplished in the hours before it's thought suitable for ladies of quality to be about. And as we're lucky enough to have neither an abundance of servants nor relatives to constrain us—since the major departs practically at dawn for his daily ride—we've adopted the habit of rising early, too. Then we immediately closet ourselves here, and for at least a few hours each day we're able to work in a most productive fashion." She frowned slightly. "Of course, I fear someone in my position shouldn't be quick to condone the sort of clandestine behavior you've just suggested, Miss Lindsay. But I confess I can't find anything truly injurious or unseemly in your proposal. And since, after all, it is for the sake of art, I collect there is little censurable—provided Elizabeth is willing—in our inviting you to join us in our morning exercises."

"Oh!" Athena exclaimed, breaking into a radiant smile. "I was very nearly certain that you wouldn't fail me!'' She flew up from her chair to hug first one and then the other.

Elizabeth, who was a good deal more reticent about displaying her emotions, looked a trifle stunned. ''I'm sure we're delighted to be of assistance,'' she said stoutly nonetheless. ''But perhaps we should discuss the particulars of our arrangement. Can you manage to have your materials sent here without attracting any great interest, do you think? Capital. Well, then, most probably you'll wish to set up your easel over here, by the window. I do hope the light will be sufficient and that my playing will not prove too distracting,'' she said anxiously, glancing toward the pianoforte on the far side of the room and then moving over to rest her hand lightly on its gleaming mahogany surface.

''Of course not. Everything will be perfect,'' Athena said in the spirit of one determined to make light of all inconveniences. ''Only consider how very comfortable we three shall be. You will work on your music and I on my painting—and Miss Palmer will guard us against all interlopers,'' she finished, enthralled at the prospect.

''And just think,'' Elizabeth continued, ''if Mr. Thurston should happen to be pleased with your painting and it becomes known, as indeed it must, that you were the painter! Then surely it wouldn't be long before you could take your pick of the numerous requests for your services from the most influential of patrons.''

She paused for breath, the rapturous look on her face giving notice that she'd been swept up in Athena's enthusiasm. Her response drew Athena to her side to clasp her hands tightly in a squeeze of pure excitement. The two young ladies regarded each other happily, both dazzled by the inevitable prospect of what remained, in fact, a far from certain future.

Athena suddenly blinked once or twice as if awakening from a doze and gave herself a shake. "Still," she said slowly after a moment, "if my initial effort were to turn out successfully, my secret will then be known. And I can scarcely credit that my aunt would be pleased to learn that I'd cozened her in such a manner, since her hopes for me lie in an altogether different direction."

"Stuff!" Miss Palmer exclaimed comfortingly. "Surely you don't think Lady Hollinwood would be slow to recognize the desirability of being related to someone whom all the world considered to be in the first style. I warrant her ladyship—once she'd recovered from the shock—would come to think your artistic talent quite to your advantage in the other area, as well."

"No doubt," Athena agreed with a grimace, her heart sinking at the notion that her ability as a painter might be counted as merely another point in her favor on the marriage mart. She hated to think that what she considered a professional calling might be seen by some as merely the amateur dabblings of yet another well-bred young lady.

"Come, now," Miss Palmer said briskly, recalling their attention with a commanding wave of her hand. "Let's leave off these fabrications for the moment, shall we, and try instead to resolve the one or two real questions that remain. For example," she continued, looking quizzically at Athena, "have you considered how you're to slip in and out of your aunt's house on the days when you mean to join us here?"

"Not entirely," Athena confessed, offering her a guilty half smile. "However, I fancy leaving will pose little difficulty, since neither my aunt nor my mother is precisely accustomed to rising early." She tilted her head to one side to consider the matter. "And as for returning, I believe I'll be able to manage that quite nicely, as well, if I take one of the household into my confidence. In fact, I know the perfect individual, and she's entirely to be trusted, I assure you."

"Admirable!" Miss Palmer exclaimed, being of a decidedly practical bent.

"Splendid!" Elizabeth exclaimed, possessing a rather more romantic nature, of which she was seldom conscious in her daily life. "Only consider, Athena dear—isn't this the most idyllic situation for an artist? You're not bound in any way whatsoever save to give form to the piece you most wish to conceive. To be sure," she concluded eagerly, "I can't wait to discover what it is you mean to do."

FORTUNATELY, Athena had never been one of those weak creatures who succumb to a fit of the vapors at the first sign of a cloud on the horizon. All the way back to Grosvenor Square she had worried at the problem of the painting, fearful that she would fail in the crucial initial decision—the choice of subject. But instead of yielding to her fears when she gained her own room—despite a strong desire to do just that—she set about completing her arrangements by ringing the bell for the young maid assigned to her service by Lady Hollinwood.

By the time the servant knocked on the door a few minutes later, Athena had assembled her painting equipment in a corner of the room and was seated composedly on the couch.

"Alice," she said pleasantly, "I have two favors to ask of you."

"Yes, miss?" Alice replied promptly, for she was rather enamored of the gentle mistress whom she often claimed to be the least demanding of all ladies.

"First," Athena said, indicating her painting box and easel, "I want these things taken to Major Stebbing's house. But I prefer them to be removed without attracting any great notice and then delivered only to Miss Stebbing herself. Can you manage that, do you think?"

"Oh, yes, miss," Alice assured her, not seeming to find anything extraordinary in this request. She tucked a stray curl beneath her cap. "Tom—the footman, you know—would be glad to do it, I fancy. He's a bit sweet on me, Tom is," she added complacently by way of explanation.

"Good. Now, then, the second thing is a trifle more difficult." Athena paused to consider how best to explain what she had in mind. "For the next several weeks I find that I shall have to leave the house for a few hours every morning. Of course, I shouldn't at all like to disturb the rest of the household. I wonder if you might show me in and out through the servant's hall so that no one but you and I need know that I've been away."

"As you wish, miss," Alice said slowly, her round blue eyes looking quite unconvinced by this reasoning.

Observing that some further inducement was required, Athena smiled and offered, "Though naturally if you're asked, you may say I'm at the Stebbings' house."

Alice, who apparently had her own opinion as to why a young lady might wish to show a light pair of heels, sniffed loudly. "Thank you, miss. But mind, if anyone smokes us out, it's likely to be me as catches the blame. And seeing as that's so," she said, planting her feet firmly, "I fancy you'd best say straight out if there's a gentleman involved."

"Certainly not!" Athena exclaimed indignantly, frowning at the disbelief on the maid's face. But appealing to Alice's romantic tendencies seemed to be the only sure way to gain her cooperation. "Well, actually," she amended, making a great show of reluctance and finding herself conveniently blushing at the same time, "there is someone. However, he's not to be involved directly in the matter, you understand. And I shall indeed be at Miss Stebbing's, in any case. Now will you help?"

"Oh, yes, miss," Alice promised. She dipped a brief curtsy, enormously gratified at having been made party to what she was now firmly convinced was a lover's tryst. "And don't let blowing the gaff to me plague you none, miss. I ain't a rattle like some I could name," she announced before bouncing proudly from the room.

ANY ILLUSION that Athena might miraculously settle the subject of the painting as readily as she had dealt with Alice seemed hopeless to her at first. None of her drawings pleased her, and she began to wonder whether her creative abilities were equal to the task.

But once she stopped her work to mull over this depressing notion, she shook her head firmly. Her trouble was that she sought not her own good opinion so much as Giles Wescott's.

Putting that thought firmly behind her, Athena examined the project again, and soon ideas began to form one after another, all fairly screaming for attention. Her fingers could scarcely relay them to paper fast enough.

In composing to please her own judgment, Athena was in fact drawing for the young lady whom Giles had described as indistinguishably resembling herself—and so, inevitably, for Giles. But perhaps it was just as well that this did not occur to her.

When she at last put down her crayons, she was rewarded by five sketches on which she could look with pride. And she felt confident that they would also be found acceptable by her two patrons.

OF COURSE, it wasn't to be hoped that such confidence would survive unchallenged. Fully two hours before Reginald Thurston's expected arrival, Athena felt herself in the grip of an unquenchable fear that her efforts would be declared wanting and her belief in her abilities misplaced.

Just as she was feeling out of sorts, Reginald was obviously very ill at ease when he appeared at the appointed hour. Athena sought to make him more comfortable and gave him such a pleasant drive with inconsequential remarks on the weather and the passing scene that he became all too aware of a prickly conscience at having agreed to deceive her in what he now saw was a truly shabby manner.

And what was more, he decided, negotiating the Grosvenor Gate and then turning down a carriage drive that ended near the Serpentine, he meant to tell the author of the plan precisely that at the first opportunity.

He soon learned that he'd be forced to postpone plain talk a little while longer. When Giles came cantering over the rise a few minutes later, Athena, who was noticeably eager to put an end to her anxiety once and for all, immediately produced her sketches. Delaying only to dismount and hand her down from the carriage, Giles just as eagerly accepted the drawings offered for his inspection and at once became engrossed in silent appraisal.

Athena stood motionless on the grass, dizzy with suspense and the tremulous sensation that had overcome her when her hand clasped his.

A full quarter hour passed without comment from any side. When Giles at last raised his head and focused on the strained face beside him, his first words caught her totally unawares.

"I collect you've been hoaxing me, Miss Lindsay. These are not the work of some neophyte requiring instruction. Dear me, no—a little counsel, perhaps, or even tutelage, if you wish. Otherwise, I confess I can't find anything much to fault," he concluded, smiling warmly into her eyes.

He savored the glow of her answering smile, which brought her face radiantly back to life, and only wished that he could wrap his arms protectively around her and keep that shining look on her face forever. He had to admit that his interest in her went considerably beyond that of a patron for an artist. But then recalling with an inward groan his role in the present scheme of things, he squared his shoulders and hurriedly revised his approach in favor of one that was less intimate.

"However, it's been my experience that what is laid down on paper frequently doesn't translate perfectly to canvas," he continued, raising his eyebrows and adopting a superior tone that he felt practically guaranteed a heated response. "Moreover, lady painters are far too commonly overpraised at the first and quite often are unable to fulfill the expectations they have raised. So you'll understand why I'll say no more at present regarding the quality of your work. I believe that judgment is best reserved for the end."

This speech fulfilled his expectations exactly. Gone was the smile and the secret and most unprofessional desire to lay her head on Giles's broad and capable shoulder. His acid remarks dispelled the rosy haze from Athena's mind and fired her with an ambition to give the lie to his casual dismissal of the labors of her entire sex.

"How disappointed you will be to learn that such is not my experience, sir," she snapped. She picked a buttercup with such force that it came out of the grass, roots and all, with a sudden jerk.

"On the contrary," he responded, steeling himself to ignore her angry glare. "I consider you fortunate not to be obliged to labor under such a handicap."

At this point, Reginald, who was altogether baffled by his companions suddenly turning on each other, broke his silence. "Shouldn't we confabulate a bit on the subject for the painting?" he inquired plaintively. "The thing is, I fear we're fast becoming a good deal too conspicuous."

"A splendid notion! I have no doubt that this will be most to your beloved's taste," Giles declared, unerringly selecting the very sketch to which Athena was most attached. He shifted his stance a trifle, the better to observe the effect of this choice.

"Excellent," Reginald exclaimed nervously, hardly pausing to glance at the drawing Giles held out to him. "I trust you've routed the other problem, as well," he asked Athena in an anxious voice.

"Yes. I've explained our situation to Elizabeth, and she has very kindly offered the loan of her house for as long as I may require it," she confirmed, turning toward him with relief, the better to avoid Giles's penetrating stare. "We mean to keep an artist's salon of sorts, you see,'' she continued in a tone of forced gaiety. ''I shall pursue my painting, and she will attend to her music—'' She broke off abruptly to peer at a vehicle that had suddenly turned in their direction. ''Why, I believe that's Elizabeth now!''

The tarnished and unfashionable landaulet heading toward them contained both Elizabeth Stebbing, who handled the lines with the ease of a country girl bred to drive all manner of conveyances, and her governess, as well.

''Miss Palmer and I found ourselves unable to resist the lure of such glorious sunshine,'' Elizabeth offered shyly after she had maneuvered her carriage beside the phaeton and greetings had been exchanged all around. ''Though had we known we'd end up in such lofty company, we might have been persuaded to reconsider our decision. I fancy our poor coach is scarcely fit to be seen in Hyde Park on the same day as yours, sir,'' she observed with such a happy disregard of her own circumstances that it brought smiles of universal approval.

As soon as Athena had allowed herself to be handed into the landaulet so that the three ladies could engage in a spirited chat, Reginald seized the opportunity to motion Giles closer and whisper accusingly, ''Mind what you're about, my boy. Though the fact is, dashed if I can even guess what you've got in the pot. Thought you meant to play the hero. After all, didn't you concoct this silly scheme to help Miss Lindsay? The next thing I know, the two of you are at dagger points. Now I ask you, does that make any sense?''

"Tush, Reggie. I've my own reasons for wanting to set Miss Lindsay on the fence.''

Reginald bent down dangerously far so that his words would be heard by no one but Giles. "Don't like this notion of yours a jot; not a jot, Giles. Didn't want to go partners in the first place. Don't want to now. What's more, it's shameful to cheat a lady,'' he declared virtuously before adding in an appreciative voice, "Regular diamond of the first water, she is, too.''

Giles was momentarily intrigued. "Do you truly think so? In any case, I can assure you it will only be to her advantage if she's known to have executed a painting on my behalf. Besides, I promise you she won't come to grief on account of it.''

"Not her reputation as a painter I'm thinking about,'' Reginald whispered tartly. "There are other considerations whenever a lady's involved. A pretty coil you've got us into, I must say. Spending all our time on this stupid bubble when by rights we should be considering how to secure your future.''

Giles wasn't about to confide that this was precisely what he was doing, and a chance remark from the other carriage saved him from having to reply.

"I beg your pardon,'' he inserted politely, wandering over to the landaulet. "Did I hear someone mention Almack's?''

"Indeed you did, sir," Elizabeth confirmed. "Athena will be making her first visit there on Wednesday."

"Really? I'll be most curious to see what you make of the place," Giles declared, throwing Athena a challenging smile.

"Oh, will you be there?" Athena asked in confusion. "From everything I've heard, I'd have thought it far too simple an amusement for you to bother about, sir."

"Yes, it's sadly slow, it's true—but utterly necessary if one intends to maintain one's standing in the polite world. I daresay," Giles said with his eye on Reginald, daring him to enter a protest, "Reggie and I will both find ourselves obliged to make a brief appearance there on Wednesday evening."

ATHENA'S PREPARATIONS for her introduction to Almack's three days later were limited by the constraints of her wardrobe, so she came downstairs to join Mrs. Lindsay in good time in her moss-green silk evening gown and her pearls. An added sparkle in her eyes gave notice that she did not intend to let Giles Wescott spoil her enjoyment of the evening.

No constraints held Lady Hollinwood, however, who changed her gown twice before settling on mauve crape with blond ruching at the neck, sleeves, waist and hem.

Her ladyship's fussings had greatly delayed the party, and by the time the barouche deposited them in St. James's and they had presented their vouchers, they found a veritable crush in the famed Assembly Rooms. The maximum number of two hundred guests had already been reached, though it was still an hour before the midnight curfew, after which the duke of Wellington himself would be denied admission.

Once her ladyship had succeeded in locating Lady Jersey and they had forced a passage to her side, the patroness devoted a bare minute to the new arrivals, merely pronouncing Athena a prettily behaved child and granting her permission to waltz; the exchange was not a memorable one.

The subsequent arrival of Major Stebbing and his daughter immediately plunged the three older members of the group into an intense discussion about the play offered in the adjoining salon. Athena was free to look around in surprise at what was nothing but a large, bare room with a rather bad floor and ropes along the sides marking off the space for dancing. Even though the room was crowded with men in the required costume of knee breeches and white cravats and women in a dazzling array of evening dress, it was clear to Athena that the music, the lighting and the company were Almack's main virtues.

She and Elizabeth were trying to discover whether any of the guests at Lady Hollinwood's party was present tonight when their attention was caught by a new arrival.

"Oh, look, there's Fanny Merivale. How I do wish I might learn to get on as she does," Elizabeth confessed wistfully, her eyes on the town's reigning beauty. "And not simply to please Papa, either. It's true that I'm content as I am, but sometimes I imagine what it must be like to be beautiful and sought after.''

"Pish!" Athena exclaimed inelegantly, linking their arms. "She may possess the form, but you, my dear Elizabeth, possess the substance." She was rewarded by a grateful smile. "Besides, I collect the lady isn't herself tonight, or why would she be hanging on that fellow's arm in such a shockingly coming way?''

Elizabeth regarded her in surprise. "Can it be you haven't heard the news? It appears that Lord Wetherford and Miss Merivale have become betrothed. I fancy you have met him. The notice was in the newspaper on Monday morning. Didn't you see it?''

"No, I didn't," Athena murmured, trying to digest the significance of this news. She was disconcerted to find that her feelings were a chaotic mixture of gladness and pain. The gladness was easy to explain, but the despondency took a minute to puzzle out, until she realized that her belief in Giles Wescott's secret betrothal had not been as firm as she had thought. She had been nursing a hope that her suspicion was unfounded, and now Miss Merivale's betrothal to another man seemed to dash that hope to pieces.

Moreover, Giles had probably known the news when they had met in the park to discuss her sketches on Monday afternoon. In her present state of mind, that appeared somehow to give him a dangerous advantage over her, so much so that she felt positively unnerved in retrospect. The ensuing stab first of anger and then of something like regret that coursed through her was so nearly physical that she blushed violently and then shuddered.

As luck would have it, Elizabeth was at that very moment watching Athena with concern. "I collect you're not feeling quite the thing," she murmured anxiously. "It is uncommonly close here tonight, and you do look a trifle feverish. Do you think perhaps something cool to drink—?"

The rest of the party all seized happily on this suggestion, particularly since the gaming room lay in the same direction as the refreshment room, and they made a push to proceed there forthwith. But having to stop and greet several of Lady Hollinwood's acquaintances along the way made their progress inevitably slow. And so it happened that turning away from one such encounter, Athena suddenly found herself face-to-face with Giles Wescott and Reginald Thurston.

Once greetings had been exchanged, Giles lost no time in soliciting Athena's hand for the waltz that was about to begin.

"Oh, do you think it advisable?" Elizabeth began, turning questioningly toward her friend. "Miss Lindsay is feeling in rather bad point at the moment," she explained, much to Athena's embarrassment.

Giles inspected Athena's flushed cheeks in disbelief. "Indeed?" he said politely, adding in a guileless tone, "I never should have guessed. But I wouldn't depend on the catlap they serve here for a restorative if I were you, Miss Lindsay. I believe the bohea alone is thought to have been the cause of at least two cases of strong hysterics."

Lady Hollinwood, who was somewhat miffed at having played no part in the conversation, at once gave a loud cackle. "Go along with you," she admonished, rapping Giles playfully on the knuckles with her fan in a flirtatious fashion. "I daresay a few turns round the room with a handsome rascal like you, Wescott, will prove to be of much better value—eh, puss?"

Now, until her aunt had spoken, Athena had been steadfastly bent on declining Giles's request, in part because her unsettled emotions had grown a good deal more turbulent since he had appeared and in part because of Lady Hollinwood's determination to throw her at his head. But just as she opened her mouth to speak, she happened to glance at him. The amusement in his eyes eloquently said that he fully understood her dilemma, and so she held out her hand to him. "Yes, I expect you're quite right, ma'am," she responded demurely.

Giles, who had been watching Athena with every appearance of being able to predict exactly the succession of thoughts passing through her mind, looked momentarily taken aback. Nevertheless, he quickly recovered his composure and proceeded to lead her out onto the dance floor.

They circled the room for some minutes in silence, both seemingly absorbed in matching the eddy and flow of the other couples, who waltzed with the fierce enthusiasm of converts to this newest import from the Continent. Athena, for her part, was wholly concentrated on her partner's hand resting on her waist, now lightly, now with increased pressure as he twirled her around. Giles, in turn, was breathing in the sweet fragrance of the dark curls that swayed just out of reach of his lips and studying Athena surreptitiously.

He was finally moved to ask in a gentle voice, "Are you truly feeling unwell?"

Athena looked up suspiciously. But the concern in his face was so obviously sincere that she felt ashamed she had doubted his honest interest in her well-being.

"I daresay it's only a passing faintness, sir," she murmured, dropping her eyes to his snowy neckcloth. "No doubt on account of the heat."

"How happy I am to hear that!" he exclaimed warmly. Then, without thinking, he promptly managed to spoil the friendly atmosphere that had been blossoming between them by adding, "I shouldn't wish you to fall prey to some dreadful malady when you're about to embark on such a very important undertaking."

On a wave of disappointment, Athena drew a full arm's length away from him. "I see I've been mistaken. Your solicitude, it seems, has more to do with my ability to fulfill my obligations than with my state of health." She fixed her eyes steadily on his. "Allow me to assure you, sir, that nothing will prevent my attempting to live up to all that is expected of me."

Giles, who had only chosen to conceal his too-personal interest with a little lightness and tact, perceived that somehow he'd made yet another mistake. He stared fixedly back at Athena, wondering how he could rescue their relationship from the misunderstandings—inadvertent and otherwise—that had plagued it from the beginning.

"Why is it," he demanded as the dance ended and he guided Athena to the side of the room, "that whenever we two meet, we inevitably take up the cudgels?"

The same question had lately been nagging at Athena, too, and she was tempted to answer that they would deal better if they were truthful with each other. But she shrank from the prospect and instead laughed up into his face and said, as a new partner stood ready to whirl her away, "I expect we're both so accustomed to managing the horses, we won't hand over the reins to anyone else to drive."

Congratulating herself on having brought this uncomfortable conversation to a close, Athena threw herself with renewed energy into the festivities. Her high spirits didn't pass without notice. While she gloried in the unaccustomed and most pleasant sensation of finding herself much sought after, laughing and exchanging witticisms with a succession of highly desirable partners, Giles withdrew silently to a corner of the room. From this vantage point he watched impassively as the slender figure in the green gown glided through a quadrille and a series of spritely country dances. And when Athena with a brilliant smile accepted an invitation to dance a second time with the handsome and very dashing Robert Vernier, a Frenchman only recently introduced to society, his brows met in a scowl.

Among the dancing, gossiping, flirting crowd, no one noticed Giles's unusual gloom save Reginald Thurston. That dedicated friend, having followed the direction of Giles's gaze, allowed himself a single exasperated sigh. Giles certainly appeared to be dangling after a woman his father would undoubtedly consider altogether unsuitable.

But then, he mused, as he watched Athena romp through an old-fashioned cotillion, what did Lord Wescott's requirements matter when his friend's happiness was at stake? Not a jot.

So when half an hour later the musicians struck up the evening's second waltz and Giles was the first to claim Athena's hand, Reginald now approved with a benevolent smile.

Yet no sooner had the couple joined in the graceful, sweeping movements of the dance than it became evident that another type of exercise had begun, as well.

"Upon my word, sir," Athena exclaimed mischievously to cover the pleasure she felt in being in his arms again, "can it be that you've returned for a second dose of my wit?"

"It seems, Miss Lindsay," Giles observed dryly, "that you're in a decidedly good humor all of a sudden."

Athena laughed. "Indeed, I'm merry as a grig, sir. Even when my father was alive and could be persuaded to escort us, few entertainments in Kent matched this one for enjoyment—or for the company, either, for that matter," she added, unconsciously gripping his hand more tightly. "Besides, since Papa wasn't disposed to let others learn who did the real work in the studio, the cosseted guest was invariably Robert Lindsay, the celebrated painter. I'm enjoying a little real attention for the first time." She leaned back slightly to search his unsmiling face. "Indeed, I think it's very mean spirited of you to destroy my pleasure."

This unanswerable attack made Giles feel that the ground had been cut away from beneath him, and he was betrayed into retorting, "That's no excuse to deport yourself like some frivolous chit."

Through sheer strong-mindedness, Athena retained the appearance of a young lady enjoying an intimate chat with the much-admired Giles Wescott. "Dear me," she murmured, "how very inconsistent you gentlemen are. I understood that such goosish behavior in a woman was irresistibly attractive to most bucks."

"I take it you're referring to Fanny Merivale," Giles said in a guarded voice, unaware of Lady Jersey's gracious nod as she twirled past. "Well, allow me to inform you that what's becoming for her doesn't in the least serve for you. She, after all, is not an artist."

How very fortunate for her, Athena thought dourly. "I hope you aren't seeking to advise me on the correct deportment for a lady painter," she resumed in a skeptical voice.

"Not precisely," Giles admitted, uncomfortably aware that this claim wasn't entirely true. "However," he continued in a desperate attempt to buttress a weak case with a specious argument, "it only makes sense that since the work of most female artists is treated so lightly, they should show through their behavior that their intentions—and therefore their paintings—are serious beyond question." He stole a measuring glance at his partner. "You can't think it advantageous for a lady painter to be accounted a simple flirt."

"No," Athena allowed, adding bluntly, "but neither do I mean to permit you, sir, merely for having secured me a commission and a temporary living, to dictate how I may conduct myself in every area of my life. And yet—" she gave an exasperated shrug that made Giles tighten his hold on her waist "—if you weren't so concerned because I'm an artist, you would undoubtedly be sermonizing simply because I'm only a female. Everyone from her mama to her husband seems bent on making a woman dance to their tune. Indeed, I should be perfectly happy to count myself a spinster—that's what I very nearly am at my advanced age. At least I'd not then have my every move subject to the dictates of a mere anybody."

"That's pitching it much too strong!" Giles exclaimed, taking this remark rather more personally than it had been intended. "I don't mean that you should take up residence in a monkery."

"I expect you mean a nunnery," Athena said kindly, regaining her good humor and eliciting a grudging smile from him. "But if you aren't bent on setting up as a right stickler, then why are you lecturing me on the niceties of address?"

Since Giles hardly knew what had caused him to take exception to Athena's quite unexceptional behavior, he was slow to respond. Could he actually be jealous? he wondered. A detestable emotion, and yet . . . He had certainly wished that Frenchman to the guillotine.

For a moment he was strongly tempted to allow the conversation to take him where it would but immediately realized that a discussion with Athena of matters a good deal more intimate than preferences in address—or in art, for that matter—was decidedly premature.

To maneuver the talk to easier ground, Giles proceeded to hang his head. "I collect," he confessed, "it must be on account of my own inglorious behavior, which causes me to become instantly aware of anyone else displaying the slightest inclination to fall from the heights of propriety."

Athena laughed. "Haven't I told you once before, sir, that acting like a lickspittle doesn't at all become you?"

"Quite possibly," he agreed. Then, hoping to switch to a safer topic, he inquired as the dance ended, "Tell me, whatever happened to Major Stebbing's request for a painting of his horse?" He put a hand to her elbow to steer her over to Elizabeth and Reginald, who were talking together a few yards away.

"Oh, now he has something altogether grander in mind," Athena replied, acquiescing. "The major desires to pose astride in full regimental toggery, as if at the moment of attack."

"Indeed," Giles said knowingly. "In the very style of the duke of Wellington. Major Stebbing much admires him, I believe."

"Oh, very much," Athena agreed. "And he's undertaken most seriously to prepare for the role. Elizabeth tells me that her father has taken to standing perfectly immobile, like a statue, and for as long as a quarter hour at a shot. She was a little alarmed at first, so you can imagine her irritation at having been put so needlessly on the fret when she discovered what he was about."

"I imagine it was the major's way of practicing to become a model model."

"Yes, and the topper was that he told Elizabeth he thought he'd soon be able to pose while asleep, if he only pegged his eyes open somehow."

Athena gave Giles a comical look that was enough to send them both off into peals of laughter.

Reginald, who'd heard only the last part of the story, smiled tolerantly. "Daresay you're both too addled to make out what a dashed good notion the old boy had," he informed them kindly. "On nights like this I've often wished for a clever way to pop off myself when some proser or other was fagging me to death. Do you think it's very difficult to learn?"

"I'm sure I couldn't tell you, Reggie," Giles replied. "But I can tell you that I want something stronger than the tea and lemonade we can get here. I think we'll go on to White's. If you'll excuse us, then?" he asked the two ladies.

Athena watched Giles and Reginald make their way slowly across the room before turning and slipping her arm through Elizabeth's. "The most provoking man," she declared, leaving no doubt in her friend's mind to whom she was referring. "One moment charming and the next insufferable. It's inevitable that we shall join issue whenever we chance to meet."

Interestingly enough, a similar judgment was voiced only a few minutes later on the street outside the club. "That's a deucedly plaguesome woman!" Giles declared emphatically. "Sometimes delightful and sometimes utterly infuriating. I'm not in the least surprised that we two always end by kicking up a row!"

CHAPTER SEVEN

NOW BEGAN WHAT ATHENA would afterward recall as one of the brightest interludes in the development of her art.

Owing to the late hour at which she had returned from Almack's, it was close on nine o'clock by the time she'd risen and dressed. She shrouded herself in the drab old pelisse and bonnet in which she had first arrived in London. Then, bundling her painting gown and smock into a packet, she crept downstairs to meet Alice.

It was on the street outside her aunt's house that the real adventure began. On her previous unescorted excursions Athena had escaped unwelcome advances; in a shabby pelisse and clutching a paper package, she was far more likely to be accosted. Although she avoided such main thoroughfares as Oxford Street and Bond Street, she was obliged first to ignore a lewd suggestion from a swaggering footman and then to avoid a young blade winding his way unsteadily home after a night's merrymaking. But instead of dampening her enthusiasm, these exchanges only served to heighten her self-confidence, so that when she arrived at Elizabeth's door ten minutes later, she was in decidedly high feather.

As soon as she set foot in Elizabeth's sitting room, the young ladies started to arrange it to their satisfaction, and before a further half hour had passed, a most harmonious scene had been established. Athena, dressed now in her paint-spotted smock, stood near the windows, preparing a large canvas propped up on her easel. Elizabeth, attired in an unfashionable breakfast robe of worn blue satin, sat at the opposite side of the room at the pianoforte, where she was endeavoring to compose a waltz. And Miss Palmer, whose clothing was at best only nondescript, reclined on a couch between them, reading Mr. Shelley's most recent epic poem, *The Revolt of Islam*.

So congenial was the atmosphere that a couple of hours slipped pleasantly by before Miss Palmer looked at the clock and advised them to bring the day's work to an end. Athena was delighted that their arrangement appeared to be succeeding fully as well as she'd hoped. Clearly the others were no less happy, for no sooner had she struggled out of her smock than she was warmly embraced first by Elizabeth and then by Miss Palmer and made to promise an earlier arrival on the morrow.

At this advanced hour, Athena's return journey to Grosvenor Square proved uneventful. Since Alice was crouched faithfully inside the rear door of Lady Hollinwood's house, waiting for her arrival, she was able to gain the safety of her bedchamber with no difficulty. But even so, after changing her gown for the third time in as many hours, she concluded wryly that she was lucky to have an excuse for her exhaustion.

This evidence that her niece had enjoyed her strenuous evening at Almack's completed Lady Hollinwood's satisfaction with the attention paid her by Giles Wescott. She first commended Athena for her exemplary behavior and then laid out plans for adding to her wardrobe in order to enlarge upon her success. Finally, she was moved to offer a few tearful reminiscences of her own prime—a sure mark of favor that she was known to bestow only rarely. The sole disquieting note was sounded by her sly hints about a certain gentleman's intentions, which made Athena fearful of what might happen if her aunt should discover that Giles Wescott's interest in her was of a distinctly different nature.

ATHENA AWOKE at just on six o'clock the following morning, and having dealt efficiently with her preparations, was able to put in an appearance at Elizabeth's only an hour later. There she spent the next several hours profitably, returning to Grosvenor Square and removing all traces of her outing by the time the rest of the household had begun to stir.

Her days soon fell into a pattern that remained virtually unaltered for the ensuing two weeks. Sometimes she wondered why it wasn't obvious to all that she was moving about in a blissful daze. She spoke only when addressed directly, she meekly accepted the flat entertainments that previously she would have scoffed at, and she conducted herself in an unusually compliant and accommodating manner. Such behavior in no way disturbed Lady Hollinwood, who privately put this change in her niece down to the whims of one who was, after all, involved in an affair of the heart.

Although she was unaware of the conclusion Lady Hollinwood had drawn, Athena quickly learned that Alice could be induced to continue to lend her aid only if continually fed the notion that she was assisting in a secret courtship. So upon her return each morning, Athena had fallen into the habit of seeming to let slip a few titbits about her imaginary lover. This risky business she invariably dismissed without much thought save for giving thanks that such a small deception was the only impediment to the execution of her plan.

NATURALLY, it wasn't to be supposed that Athena's new existence would proceed without any interruptions whatsoever. The most important of these took place five days after she'd begun the painting and proved to be of a rather disturbing nature. It began innocently enough with Mrs. Lindsay asking her daughter to accompany her to a haberdasher's.

To Athena's surprise, once they were settled in her aunt's elegant barouche, Mrs. Lindsay gave the appearance of being ill at ease. She teased nervously at a loose thread on one of her gloves and bit her lower lip in the characteristic way that always indicated she'd fallen prey to some annoyance.

"Is there anything in particular you wish to speak to me about, Mama?" Athena at last prodded gently.

"Oh, no. Well, that is, yes, perhaps—" Mrs. Lindsay exclaimed confusedly. She paused for a moment and then inquired suddenly, "You are enjoying your visit here, are you not, my love?"

"Oh, enormously," Athena assured her. "It has quite exceeded my expectations."

"How glad I am to hear you say so, for you see, those are precisely my sentiments, too," Mrs. Lindsay confessed, smiling happily. "Indeed, my only reluctance to come here had to do with your plan to become a painting instructress, since as you know, I never liked the idea of deceiving Louisa in such an unseemly way." She smoothed her black spencer over her round little figure.

"Yes, yes, I remember," Athena said soothingly. "But you may be quite comfortable on that head. I've since determined to give up the matter altogether," she explained quite truthfully.

Mrs. Lindsay appeared considerably relieved. "Well, I daresay that's entirely for the best. For truly Louisa has been everything that is kind—getting up a party in our honor, escorting us to Almack's and to the opera and providing us with all manner of entertainments."

"So you've found our experiment to be a pleasant one, Mama."

"Oh, it has been immensely enjoyable," Mrs. Lindsay confessed. "And ever since I have come to understand the pleasures of card play, I find that

Louisa and I are entirely companionable. In point of fact— Well, that is to say—your aunt has been so obliging as to invite me to extend my stay in town indefinitely.''

This news had Athena goggling at her mother in astonishment, her mouth indelicately at half cock. Until that moment, she'd privately felt that her aunt, though she had been generous in the way of clothes and parties, had a precise notion of the considerable expense required to provide for the two additions to her household. Moreover, Lady Hollinwood obviously had a very low opinion of her sister-in-law's mental capacity.

Even the uninquiring Mrs. Lindsay couldn't fail to observe Athena's reaction. However, she clearly misunderstood its origin, because she now clasped her hands earnestly together and added hastily, ''Of course, you are invited to remain as well, love.''

''Of course,'' Athena agreed unsteadily, daunted by the shifts she'd have to practice to escape that dismal prospect. But seeing that her mother was still looking at her expectantly, she pulled herself together and said affectionately, ''A most unexpected proposal, is it not, Mama? I'm heartily glad that my aunt has had such a sensible idea. Town life suits you to perfection. You wouldn't have been happy to bury yourself in Kent.''

FOR THE REMAINDER of the day Athena found herself unable to dismiss Lady Hollinwood's suggestion that the Lindsays consider her house in Grosvenor Square their home, and it kept her awake that night.

The offer was altogether in Mrs. Lindsay's best interests, for she had fairly blossomed in their new environment.

But Athena was a good deal less certain about how her aunt's proposal might affect her own plans. The number of occasions on which she'd chafed at Lady Hollinwood's well-meaning but inopportune meddling in her affairs was past counting. Yet even the prospect of continuing to reside under her protection might be preferable to the other avenues open to a lady of limited expectations—preferable, Athena admitted to herself, were it not for the disturbing presence of Giles Wescott, whose proximity was beginning to cause her such emotional unrest.

Her thoughts whirled about in her brain like a Catherine wheel, so it wasn't surprising that she suffered an uneasy night. And when, an hour after her arrival at Elizabeth's, even the soothing atmosphere of her studio corner and the demands of her painting had failed to dissolve the curious melancholy that had settled on her, she threw down her brush in frustration and exclaimed disgustedly, "Damnation!"

"Can it be that you're having some difficulty with your work, my love?" Elizabeth inquired hesitantly.

"If only I were!" Athena declared with feeling. Conscious of an overwhelming exhaustion, she pulled off her smock and cast herself down on the sofa beside Miss Palmer. "No—no reverses with the painting, thank heaven. Though I fancy that it has everything to do with painting," she said slowly as if to herself. "You see, my aunt has offered to give Mama and me a home for as long as we might wish."

"But that is beyond anything great!" Elizabeth cried. "And here I've been wondering this age how I could ever get on without you. Though naturally," she added quickly, shrinking a little on her stool, "I realize you may not have reason to feel as strongly as I do."

Athena, who had long since come to regard Elizabeth as nearly a sister, hastened to reassure her. "Nothing of the sort. Why, I consider our friendship to be the happiest outcome of my stay in London. After all, you and Miss Palmer are the very first ladies of my acquaintance who don't consider my pursuits odd."

Elizabeth smiled happily at Athena. "Then I fear I don't see what you find objectionable about Lady Hollinwood's proposal."

Athena shifted restlessly about on the sofa before replying. "It's only that I can't be convinced that my fortune will be assured solely by this one painting," she blurted out. "It's too fantastical to imagine that it will be. And if it isn't, then I'll be in precisely the same position that I was in before I undertook the commission."

A brief silence ensued as the three ladies considered this depressing prospect.

"Didn't you tell us, my dear," Miss Palmer inquired briskly, "that one of your intentions in coming to London was to discover whether you could obtain some artistic instruction for yourself?" Athena nodded. "Well, then, suppose you were accepted in some well-known artist's studio, or even at the Royal Academy. In either event, I imagine your chances for success would be vastly improved, wouldn't they? And I take it that you've therefore made the appropriate inquiries."

"Well, actually, you see, I haven't yet found the opportunity to do so," Athena confessed awkwardly, squirming a little under that steady gaze.

"And yet you've already seen fit to despair of your future?" Miss Palmer exclaimed in an incredulous tone. "Really, child, I should think very poorly of you if you failed to explore all possibilities before reaching such a momentous conclusion.

"Now, then, let's go about the thing in an orderly way, shall we?" She rose and began walking around the room, a system she always found conducive to good thinking. "Firstly, I imagine we should determine which persons would prove most helpful to approach, and secondly you should endeavor to secure appointments with them." Her two companions regarded her expectantly. "Now, as far as the former is concerned," she went on in a practical tone, "I daresay you should consult Mr. Wescott for advice, since as a collector he will have considerable knowledge of painters and studios."

"Just the thing!" Elizabeth exclaimed, gazing admiringly at her governess.

"Certainly not!" Athena exclaimed in dismay, blushing furiously. "I tell you I will not be induced to consult that man about my private affairs. He has taken far too great an interest in them already.''

That unguarded remark having aroused her companions' curiosity, she allowed herself the luxury of revealing the whole of her suspicions to them.

"So you see why," she concluded a few minutes later, sinking back tiredly against the sofa, "I've every reason to believe that the painting on which I'm now working is not intended for Mr. Thurston at all but for Mr. Giles Wescott instead."

Another silence followed as her audience digested the significance of Athena's story. "Do you mean to say, then, that it is Mr. Wescott himself who is secretly betrothed?" Elizabeth asked slowly, having fitted together the pieces of the puzzle.

"Exactly. And in view of the fact that rather than taking me into his confidence on that score, he has instead put together this ridiculous fabrication and actually expected me to believe it, I certainly won't beg him for any help. Unfortunately," she continued, pushing her fingers through her tangled hair and failing to meet their eyes, "I must also tell you that—that I let my affections become engaged before I learned of this deception and his prior commitment. So I now find myself in the position of having given my heart to a man whose own is clearly... elsewhere."

A sidelong glance between Miss Palmer and Elizabeth showed that they had both reached the same conclusion about why Athena wished to avoid Giles Wescott and why continuing to reside with her aunt would not suit her.

Miss Palmer merely said, "Just as you wish, my dear. Besides, I'm convinced you're quite right to insist that we rely on our own devices instead of depending on favors solicited from others. Therefore, if you've no objections, I shall undertake to discover whom it would be most beneficial for you to visit."

"I'd be most obliged if you would," Athena said in a relieved voice. "And I promise that I'll make every effort to turn that information to advantage."

Conversation came to a temporary halt, for the three ladies found themselves rather worn down by the these emotional revelations. At last Elizabeth looked curiously at her friend. "And what does your mama think of Lady Hollinwood's invitation, I wonder."

"Oh, she confessed to me that she found it entirely appealing," Athena admitted. "And indeed, why would she feel otherwise? Here in town she has met with an unqualified success. She's been welcomed into my aunt's circle in such a warm and flattering fashion that she'd have to be the most unfeeling creature alive not to be delighted at her new existence. And that's precisely what renders my position so very difficult, since I shouldn't wish my feelings in any way to influence her new happiness." She started to scrape at a blob of yellow paint on her thumb.

"The fact is," she continued in a worried tone, "I'd have said that Mama had nearly forgotten our former life altogether if it weren't for her reaction to the letter she received yesterday from my father's former assistant. It appears that Mr. Pennington plans to come to town next week to order some new painting materials. And he also writes that he proposes to pay us the honor of calling in Grosvenor Square." She wrinkled her brow with distaste. "I do hope he doesn't mean to tease Mama with some pettiness or other, though it would be quite like him to do so. I believe I've never met a man as insensitive as he is to the feelings of others—as I've every reason to know."

This speech appeared to have consumed the remainder of Athena's strength, for she took her leave not long afterward.

Elizabeth remained staring thoughtfully across the room for some time following her friend's departure. Then she rose and took several deep, steadying breaths.

"I wish to pay a morning call, Lucy," she announced without any preamble, "and I'd like you to bear me company."

Miss Palmer looked at her charge with some surprise. "Of course, love," she said pleasantly. "And may I be permitted to learn whom we're to visit?"

"You may. I intend to call upon Mr. Reginald Thurston. I have in mind to speak with him about a matter of some importance."

"No, you most certainly will not!" Miss Palmer cried in a shocked tone. "Why, such an act would hold your reputation up to serious question. Besides, you know perfectly well that it's quite improper for a lady of quality to visit a gentleman alone in his quarters."

"Just the same, I'm going," Elizabeth said defiantly, though with a catch in her voice. "And at any rate, I shan't be alone with him, since you'll be there, too. What's more, it's not as if I will enjoy the experience. You know how much I hate paying calls.''

''Then you do see—''

''I only see,'' Elizabeth interrupted, ''that it won't serve for me to be cowardly when what I have in mind may save a dear friend much unhappiness. Surely you agree that in such a case I have a veritable duty to force myself to pay the visit, however much I may shrink from it.'' She drew herself up to her full height of five feet. ''I shall simply resolve to be firm and matter-of-fact, and everything will turn out splendidly, I'm sure,'' she finished in a brave voice. She gave her governess a conciliatory hug. ''But pray don't oppose me in this matter. It's utterly necessary, I assure you, or I shouldn't even think of doing it.''

''Oh, very well,'' Miss Palmer sniffed. ''But I warn you, I cannot like it.''

''No,'' Elizabeth agreed readily, beginning to search through a pile of miscellaneous articles for her gloves. ''But then, I daresay we'll very likely find that Mr. Thurston shares your sentiments exactly.''

ELIZABETH PROVED to be entirely correct. However, Reginald was able to disguise the shock he felt with the address for which he was rightly famous. Despite having risen only two hours earlier and being called from his breakfast still attired in a dressing gown of red China silk, he struggled into his coat and welcomed the callers into a sitting room smothered in gilt and lacquer and crowded with his collection of snuffboxes as calmly as if their arrival were a mere commonplace.

First settling them in a pair of elaborate green-painted Trafalgar chairs and offering to ring for some refreshments, he seated himself opposite. Then, looking from one to the other, he politely begged how he could be of service.

Now that she was actually confronted by the object of her quest, Elizabeth was suddenly conscious of doubting the wisdom of what she meant to propose. But reminding herself not to shilly-shally, she straightened in her chair and stared her host directly in the eye.

"Sir," she demanded abruptly, "are you or are you not betrothed?"

"Yes!" Reginald replied promptly. "Well, at least, that is—" He sucked his lips together quickly.

"What?" Elizabeth demanded.

"Can't tell. That is to say, won't. Gave my word of honor I shouldn't."

"It seems to me," Elizabeth declared tartly, "that there may be more important things at stake here, sir, than your honor."

Reginald thrust his head forward like a tortoise from its shell and regarded her as if he weren't certain he'd heard correctly. "Nothing as essential as the honor of a gentleman," he assured her in a profound voice.

"Not even the happiness of your dearest friend?" Elizabeth objected. "Especially when it might be within your power to assist in securing it?"

"How?" he inquired cautiously, this plea having hit nearer the mark.

"Let's settle the other matter first, if you please," Elizabeth said in a firm voice. "You are not engaged to be married?"

Reginald shook his head vigorously. "No. All Giles's idea, you see. Said he wanted to help Miss Lindsay. Said she wouldn't accept a commission from him directly. Dreamed up this nonsensical scheme instead. Didn't want to do it. Not fitting to deceive a lady. Don't know what possessed Giles. Don't know what possessed me to agree. Still, very persuasive fellow, Giles."

"Indeed," Elizabeth said briefly, for she'd already begun to formulate the reason for Giles's actions, even if Reginald clearly had not. "But at any rate, that charade was all to no purpose," she informed him a trifle heartlessly. "Athena never believed the painting was meant for you at all." She hesitated. "You're quite certain that Mr. Wescott concocted this whole stratagem merely to afford her some temporary employment? It isn't perhaps he who is secretly betrothed?"

"Certainly not!" Reginald declared, adding in a conspiratorial tone, "The fact is, I've thought on occasion that Giles was trying to fix his interest with Miss Lindsay. Hope it wasn't anything in my conduct that caused you to think Giles was intending to post the banns?"

"It's not I who thinks so," Elizabeth said, becoming bolder by the minute. "It's Athena who thinks so. You see, Mr. Wescott has captured her affections."

"Oh," Reginald said. "Oh!" he repeated in a more agitated voice as the implication of this revelation became clear. "I knew that cursed plan of his wouldn't fadge," he bleated. "Told Giles we'd end up in the mud—and so we damnably have. Whatever are we to do?" he pleaded, rolling his eyes anxiously at his guests.

"That," Elizabeth said with patience, "is precisely what we're here to discuss. After all, if our two friends have been so misguided as to have let themselves be swept into dangerous waters, it's our task—if not our sacred obligation—to throw them a line. Don't you agree?"

Reginald leaped up and looked as though he would bolt from the room. "No! Giles wouldn't like it—I promise he wouldn't. Told and retold me that he don't wish to find me taking an interest in his affairs. What's more, I mean to do as he says. Got a terrible manner when he's crossed, you know."

Elizabeth gave him a charitable look. "Now I understand. It isn't that you don't wish to help but only that you're too fainthearted. Of course, I'm quite aware that I, for example, normally seem a most timorous person. And yet I'd never be so poor spirited as to allow the possibility of incurring Athena's displeasure dissuade me from attempting something that I believed to be for her benefit. Still," she added in a burst of generosity, "I fully understand your reluctance to do likewise, sir."

"Didn't say I wouldn't," he corrected her sulkily, "but dashed if I see how I'm to force Giles to do anything that grates on his ear."

"Not force him. But you must try to persuade him. All I'm suggesting," Elizabeth pointed out in a reasonable voice, "is that you let slip to Mr. Wescott that we believe Athena loves him. You will simply be providing him with information. He may do what he likes with it."

"Suppose I could manage that," Reginald conceded. "I must say, though, that Giles seems queerly slow all of a sudden to seek out Miss Lindsay's company."

"Yes. Athena appears to shrink from meeting him, as well. But I think she and Mr. Wescott will be obliged to meet—out of necessity—once the painting's completed, which I believe will be in about one week. At the same time I'm told a certain Mr. Pennington may be expected to call at Grosvenor Square, the same Mr. Pennington who was formerly Mr. Lindsay's assistant, and Athena's most tenacious suitor besides. I'm sure that the gentleman means to renew his suit as soon as he arrives in town. What better occasion can we pick for your friend to seek an interview with mine? I warrant that jealousy will accomplish much that reason and prudence cannot." She sighed romantically.

"You're sadly mistaken if you think Giles would count some nobody of a rustic a serious rival," Reginald informed her scornfully.

"That may be so, sir," Elizabeth replied, recalled abruptly to her purpose. "But even so, more than one man has succeeded precisely because no one believed he could. We would be fools if we allowed that scene to play without interruption."

"I daresay you've hit the thing fair and square, after all," Reginald said glumly. "What do you wish me to do?"

"Do you mean to say that you approve of the notion?" Elizabeth exclaimed in surprise. Observing by her host's expression that she was clearly straining the point, she continued hastily. "I fancy there's nothing much to attend to at present, sir. Your part will come once the painting has been completed, for whatever may be Athena's suspicions concerning its true owner, she cannot do otherwise than formally present the work to you. And that, as you've probably already guessed," she went on encouragingly, "will afford you the perfect opportunity to convey to Mr. Wescott not only his property but also the vital information about Mr. Pennington's visit."

"But suppose she don't succeed in finishing the thingummy before that cursed fellow arrives?" Reginald objected nervously with a rare stroke of logic.

"You may safely leave that problem to me. If necessary, I shall point out to Athena the advantages of disposing of the commission as quickly as possible. Now we have but to learn the precise date of Mr. Pennington's arrival before setting our plan in motion. In the meantime, sir,'' Elizabeth said, rising to her feet, ''allow me to thank you again for your pledge of support. I'm certain Mr. Wescott will want to thank you himself, once he's been apprised of the role you've played.''

Reginald shuddered. ''Only if it turns up trumps,'' he pointed out fretfully, ''and even then, I wonder.''

On that inauspicious note the two ladies departed.

But once they were on their way home in a hack, Miss Stebbing's newfound courage seemed all at once to desert her. ''Oh, Lucy,'' she said with a sigh, ''what if this plan of ours should fail to bear fruit? Whatever will Athena do then?''

IN KEEPING with her promise, Miss Palmer obtained the names of three gentlemen upon whom it seemed advantageous for Athena to call. Athena screwed up her courage and duly wrote to all three and was surprised to obtain an interview with every one of them. She immediately became intensely apprehensive.

Her meeting with Mr. John Varley, founder of the Old Water-Color Society, was not calculated to lay her fears to rest. He greeted Athena politely enough and even condescended to examine the sketches she offered, albeit with a notable lack of enthusiasm. However, his comments were of such a sly and insinuating nature that he seemed to be expressing appreciation of her appearance rather than of her work. But most curious of all was his reaction when Athena finally inquired in a timid voice whether she might join the society. He gave her a very skeptical look and began to question her about her familiarity with various well-known gentlemen in town.

Her second call, upon Charles Leslie of the private club known as the Sketching Society, proved equally unproductive but a good deal more enlightening. He began by running down a list of noble ladies and asking her in a dubious tone whether she had actually been introduced to them. True, Athena had imagined that a certain degree of curiosity about her background and situation was to be expected. But when Mr. Leslie scarcely vouchsafed a glance at her drawings before asking her with a grin how long she had been acquainted with Mr. Giles Wescott, a grim suspicion began to form in her mind.

It was unhappily confirmed during Athena's final visit, this one to the president of the Royal Academy, Benjamin West. Unlike the other two gentlemen, Mr. West at least gave the appearance of having a real interest in her work. But her request that she be permitted to study at the academy was met with a third cool and unequivocal refusal. Even a young lady as well connected as Miss Lindsay must be denied admission to that revered institution, Mr. West said. Faced with a blank look, he then went so far as to inform Athena bluntly that a lady of her type would have been better off to take her protector Mr. Wescott's word for it rather than place herself in the compromising position of being obliged to hear a refusal from him directly.

Athena walked back to Grosvenor Square blind to her surroundings and overcome by a choking rage at the one man she could now identify as the agent of all her difficulties. That Giles Wescott should have made any inquiries on her behalf without first seeking her consent was intolerable. So what if he had done so to advance her career? He had no right to speak for her. And now his high-handed interference had laid her open to disreputable suggestions. The memory of Varley's sly looks and West's cutting civility flooded her face with color.

He hadn't even had the honesty to admit to her that he had approached the three men and failed. And it was precisely this omission that had just condemned her to repeat the round of calls that he himself had already paid. How brazen she must have appeared! And how utterly ridiculous!

It seemed to Athena that Giles Wescott had not overlooked a single opportunity to meddle in her concerns—and with uniformly calamitous results. First he'd deceived her at Ackermann's, then he'd tricked her into accepting his commission, and now he'd confounded her with the three most influential art groups in London and damaged her reputation.

The thought did cross her mind that had he refrained from taking a hand in her life, she might have found her visit to London very flat. And that acknowledgment once again stirred up in her emotions that reflected a good deal more favorably on the gentleman in question. Without a doubt, the inner workings of her heart were in a hopelessly turbulent state.

CHAPTER EIGHT

PROPPED UP on her mound of pillows, Lady Hollinwood vigilantly bent an ear to catch the sound of her niece's door closing. She had only the preceding week become aware quite by accident of similarly mysterious comings and goings.

Waking one morning some two hours earlier than usual, she had paid a surprise visit to Athena's chamber only to discover that its occupant was unaccountably missing. She had fussed nervously around her own room until some hours later when Athena's door shut quietly again. No doubt, her ladyship told herself, Athena had been out on some easily explained errand.

Nevertheless, Lady Hollinwood's morning slumbers had become a good deal less restful since then, particularly once she discerned a pattern in these absences, which occurred with suspicious regularity. So far casual inquiries had failed to provide a satisfactory explanation. Now Lady Hollinwood was finally moved to act by a fear that Athena might be the target of some havey-cavey business.

It was with this thought in mind that she rang the bell for Alice, determined to learn the whys and wherefores of the matter without further delay.

Lady Hollinwood began by inquiring how Alice was dealing with her young mistress.

"Oh, she's prime, Miss Lindsay is!" Alice exclaimed. "She always remembers to give me a bit of a smile for my trouble."

"Humpf," Lady Hollinwood declared with a sniff at this confirmation of her niece's good breeding. "Still, I daresay you must find her interminable excursions a trifle tiresome—?" she asked in a kinder tone. "No? You don't have more pressing claims on your time than dancing attendance on my niece every morning at such a very unusual hour? I take it she goes out walking."

"Yes, m'lady," Alice agreed guardedly.

"I wonder where?" Lady Hollinwood mused as if to herself. "But then doubtless you can enlighten me in that regard...."

"Well," Alice offered cautiously, "she did tell me she went visiting Miss Stebbing, m'lady."

"Gammon!" Lady Hollinwood exclaimed in a scornful voice. "Surely you ain't thinking I'll swallow that tale. What could compel a lady to go traipsing over to another lady's day after day I'm sure I couldn't say." She sat upright in bed and leaned forward in a way that made Alice shuffle her feet uncomfortably. "Now listen well, my girl," she warned in dire accents. "I won't take an unduly harsh view of your deplorable behavior if you tell me this instant what you know of this business.''

"But I don't know anything for certain, m'lady,'' Alice protested.

"Come, come,'' Lady Hollinwood snapped.

"Well, m'lady,'' Alice mumbled at last, "I did ofttimes wonder if she mightn't be meeting a gentleman.''

"Who?'' Lady Hollinwood demanded, seizing on this morsel as she might a particularly delectable piece of pheasant pie.

"That's just what I don't rightly know, m'lady. And that's the real simon-pure of it, I promise!''

"Ha!'' her ladyship exclaimed, favoring her servant with a piercing look. "Yes, I'm satisfied you truly don't know. But do you mean to say my niece has never spared so much as a word about this gentleman?''

"You mean like what each of 'em said and what he looks like and such?'' Alice asked. "Oh, yes, indeed she did,'' she admitted, and proceeded to relate every one of the bits of information that Athena had supplied to her during the past few weeks.

Only once Lady Hollinwood felt certain that the last possible titbit had been gleaned from Alice did she finally dismiss her and settle back once more against her pillows. In point of fact, she was anxious to be alone with her thoughts, which the interview had stirred into an altogether muddy stew.

Everything in Alice's story pointed to only one conclusion: Her niece had described to a hair the distinctive appearance and matchless address of a certain gentleman whom anyone of the least understanding would easily be able to name.

That Giles Wescott should turn out to be the person whom Athena was tripping out to meet was not in itself perhaps so surprising, her ladyship mused. She lifted a hand to straighten the Belgian lace cap that had slipped to one side during her interview with Alice. But that Athena had apparently consented to behave in such a hoydenish fashion was somewhat more so—particularly since she herself was in constant expectation of receiving his application to pay formal court to her niece.

Something untoward must have occurred to have persuaded Athena to trade an unsoiled reputation for the dubious and transitory pleasures of a mere dalliance. But what that event might have been, Lady Hollinwood was quite at a loss to say. Athena would never willingly have entered into such a scheme, she was sure. The very thought made her so faint that she was obliged to revive herself with a cup of chocolate. No, she decided, this must have been a wicked take-in. Men, after all, were notoriously impatient to dispense with the proprieties. And that being the case, wouldn't it be more productive instead of questioning her niece to confront Mr. Wescott directly? If he could thereby be compelled to accept the blame for placing Athena's character under suspicion, mightn't he also be persuaded to rectify that mistake by making her an offer of marriage?

So impressed was her ladyship by her own reasoning that she checked the impulse to set off forthwith only with some difficulty. In the end she decided to postpone any movement on her part until further study of Athena's activities enabled her to fix on the most auspicious time for the interview.

Her ladyship then spent the remainder of the morning congratulating herself that her good sense would shortly see the betrothal of her niece to the only son of Herbert Wescott—who was, she recalled with a sigh, a rather prime catch himself in her day.

LORD WESCOTT'S legitimate heir was at that very moment seated in his study, congratulating himself on having just completed a letter whose salutation read, "My dear Miss Lindsay." He was fond of this light, spacious room and looked forward to introducing Athena to his favorite pictures: a luminous Constable watercolor, which hung over the marble fireplace, and Angelica Kauffmann's *Portrait of Goethe*, which dominated the opposite wall.

"Hullo, dear fellow," Reginald said in a friendly way, wandering into the room on the heels of Giles's butler and draping his frame negligently over a chair without awaiting an invitation. "Deuced uncomfortable seat, this!" He shifted to an old wing chair near Giles's desk.

"Yes, isn't it?" Giles said with a sympathetic smile. "Chippendale, though."

"Oh. Different story entirely," Reginald conceded. "You ain't writing your memoirs, are you, Giles?"

"What—? Oh, I beg your pardon, Reggie," his friend said with a guilty start. "I'm afraid my mind's elsewhere at the moment."

"Don't consider it," Reginald begged him politely. "Daresay I chose a poor time to come calling. Though maybe there's some way I can be of assistance?"

"I rather think not. I've been composing a note to Miss Lindsay."

This revelation caused Reginald's interest to quicken appreciably. "Indeed?" he asked in what he hoped was a casual voice.

"Yes. Merely a line or two requesting an interview with her at some convenient time."

Excellent, Reginald thought. "But why write it down at all?" he asked. "Don't fancy you need to stand on ceremony with Miss Lindsay. Always thought myself she didn't relish such niceties."

"As did I," Giles agreed. "But the thing is—" He rose from his chair and began to stride about the room to vent an excess of nervous energy. "If only I hadn't been such a cursed stick at the first. And then to have compounded the error by foolishly deciding not to let my true feelings show—"

"Your feelings?" Reginald prompted delicately.

"No doubt you've observed that my attentions toward Miss Lindsay have become rather marked of late?" his friend inquired somewhat impatiently.

"Yes, must say the notion had occurred to me. But in any case," Reginald forged on, determined to do his duty, "the lady shows a decided preference for your company, as well."

"Precisely what I thought," Giles agreed, fetching up in front of the fire. "She's everything I ever wished for in a wife and yet never really hoped to find. Someone with whom I needn't conceal my real interests, because she shares them, too. A woman who seeks to use her life for more than merely frivolous pursuits. And yet, at the same time, one whose honeyed words seem perfectly capable of leading me, all neat and trusting, into one mishap after another." His eyes crinkled in remembered amusement. "In point of fact," he concluded a trifle apologetically, "I'm afraid Miss Lindsay has altogether captured my heart."

"Capital!" Reginald was a good deal relieved to find he'd assessed the extent of his friend's affections to the inch. "Think the two of you are perfectly suited myself. Only do alight now, dear fellow. You're making my head ache bobbing about like some deuced jack-in-the-box."

Giles cast himself obediently down on the nearest seat. "The thing is," he began again, "I told you myself that she said she'd be happy to be counted a spinster."

"Thought that was just a figure of speech," his friend objected. "Besides, heat of the battle, as I recall."

"Quite," Giles allowed. He rubbed one hand absentmindedly over the marble bust next to his chair. "But in any case, what the lady said ain't greatly to the point. It's what she hasn't yet said that concerns me. I don't even know if there's anyone else in the wings or if some other damned fellow might not already have asked for her hand. That's why I thought to write and request an interview, you see. I should be able to discover what her feelings for me really are quite easily, and then I can make my own known to her with like ease."

He paused for a moment to study the dubious expression on his friend's face. "No, you're right." he said dejectedly before Reginald could open his mouth. "The whole notion's as hollow as a honey tree. I wonder why I didn't see it till now? She might refuse to see me even if I do send around a proper note, and even if she does have a tenderness for me, she's hardly likely to declare it spontaneously."

Giles sat forward on the edge of his chair and examined his friend in the calculating way Reginald had come to recognize boded nothing but ill for him. "No," Giles repeated enthusiastically, "far better if I wait until you make a few inquiries into Miss Lindsay's situation on my behalf. You can ask... Yes, I'm sure Miss Stebbing would be willing to assist us. Her friend's happiness is at issue, too. Do you think you know Miss Stebbing well enough to call on her and extract her knowledge of Miss Lindsay's feelings for me?"

"Mere social acquaintances," Reginald pointed out, fighting a rearguard action. "Scarcely qualifies us to discuss such personal details."

"But you do agree," Giles said, mowing him down with logic, "that knowing what direction the wind's blowing in before I seek an interview with Miss Lindsay would vastly improve my chances, don't you?"

Reginald nodded reluctantly. "Then surely you must see that I have no recourse but to depend on you to discover it."

To forestall any more objections, Giles sprang up again and shook his friend's hand warmly. "You won't spoil my lay, I know. Why, you're the very soul of discretion."

"I don't doubt that I am," Reginald agreed unsteadily. "But do you truly think—"

"And don't delay," Giles continued urgently. "I collect a few more days will see the end of Miss Lindsay's labors and likewise put the period to the more intimate aspect of our relationship."

"Oh, you may depend on me," Reginald promised quite truthfully, "to help you set the seal on your courtship almost at the very moment the last stroke is laid on the painting."

SOME THREE DAYS after the preceding conversation took place, Athena completed her painting. Not unnaturally, perhaps, the effect was somewhat anticlimactic. One moment she was still adding a dab of color here or a highlight there, and the next she was unable to locate a single place on the canvas that called for additional work.

"You seem to have reached the consummation of your labors, love," Elizabeth said tentatively. "As for myself, I confess that the end of any such hard-won contest always throws me into the most unaccountably poor spirits." She came to stand at Athena's shoulder and view the finished picture. "I do so hope that you haven't similarly been struck low?"

"But that is precisely what has happened," Athena admitted slowly. "Though I'm sure I never thought I'd feel so beset by such a nonsensical feeling of loss." She wiped her hands on a rag and tossed it down with an air of finality.

This confession having restored her sense of proportion, Athena was able to turn to packing her materials and to arranging for the transfer of the painting to its new owner. However, since the second matter also affected Elizabeth's plans, a lively discussion at once ensued concerning how best to handle that exchange. Indeed, in the end, Miss Palmer found it necessary to intervene.

Might Athena not consider sending a note to Mr. Thurston by one of the Stebbings' servants, advising him that the painting had been completed and so passing the initiative onto him?

Persuaded by the convenience of this argument, Athena allowed pen and paper to be placed at hand and settled herself to compose an appropriate message.

"Do you know, I won't be surprised now if I find myself fatigued out of all patience in short order," she declared brightly as she sealed the note. "I've nothing whatsoever to anticipate in the coming weeks—save perhaps the prospect of confounding Horace Pennington's aspirations when he arrives two days hence."

At this piteous remark, Elizabeth, who only a moment before had been in a fever of anxiety to see her friend depart, enveloped Athena in a sisterly embrace. "You mustn't forget that you're always welcome to take refuge here with us, love."

Athena hugged her back. "Yes, it's not as if we'll never clap eyes on one another again. Even though it won't be quite the same."

When Athena had gone, Elizabeth sat looking at the note she had left on the writing table as distastefully as though it were a dead mouse. But by imagining in vivid detail some of the more dreadful alternatives available to Athena if she lacked the courage to carry out her plan, Elizabeth got up her nerve and strode over to the table. She boldly tore open the seal, and after scanning the brief message, dipped pen in ink and proceeded to add a few lines to the contents. That act appeared to please her enormously, for she turned to her companion and exclaimed with a satisfied smile, "Now we shall see, Lucy!"

THE LADIES' CONFIDENCE in Reginald's ability to execute his part in their scheme survived their interview with him, although not without being severely threatened. At first he strongly objected to conveying the painting and the information about Horace Pennington's arrival to Giles immediately. After all, he pointed out, if the fellow wasn't alighting for two days yet, what was to prevent Giles on hearing the whole of the story, from attempting to seek out Miss Lindsay straightaway? Upon being reminded by Elizabeth that

it was incumbent on him to keep to the plan and prevent any hitches, Reginald then protested that he was
merely exercising a modicum of discretion so that they
shouldn't be found out. It was only after Elizabeth
had cautioned him sternly not to mistake pluckless-
ness for prudence that he was persuaded to hoist his
considerable burden and depart.

Elizabeth wasn't altogether convinced that they
could rely on Reginald's courage, but she was comforted by Miss Palmer's reminder that a gentleman, as
Reginald himself was so fond of repeating, was above
all subject to the dictates of honor. No matter how
much he disliked it, Mr. Thurston would surely keep
his word. Of that, they agreed at last, they might at
least be certain.

UNHAPPILY FOR HIM, Reginald's adherence to the
word of a gentleman was fully as inviolable as the two
ladies believed. A nice appreciation for his reputation, coupled with an exact sense of responsibility,
caused him to present himself a short while later at
Giles's house, the troublesome painting in tow.

Giles brightened visibly at his entrance. "You've
seen Miss Stebbing, then, I take it?" he demanded
eagerly at once. "And brought some word regarding
Miss Lindsay? Well, out with it, man. Don't hang fire
now!" he implored.

Much to his surprise, Reginald responded to this
plea by promptly leaving the study. He reappeared
holding Athena's painting before him like a shield and

staggered across the room to deposit the piece triumphantly at his friend's feet.

Giles's first response was a startled "Upon my
word!" at being so summarily presented with at least
a portion of what he sought. Then his professional
curiosity took charge. Moving the painting to where
it caught the light from the windows, he began to
study it with an intensity softened neither by Reginald's attempts to claim his attention nor by the passage of time. Nearly a quarter hour slipped by before
he at last raised his head and exclaimed with marked
satisfaction, "Dashed if she hasn't carried it off!"

Now Reginald had been pleasantly contemplating
the modest praise he expected to receive for having
faithfully executed his part in his friend's scheme.
Consequently, he was heard to mumble crossly and
not entirely under his breath, "I had nothing whatsoever to do with the enterprise, of course. Doubtless
the cursed thing would have turned up eventually
without my taking a hand."

Giles immediately looked a good deal chastened.
"Dear me," he ventured after a moment in penitent
accents, "what a very ill-tutored fellow I've become.
I must beg your pardon, Reggie, for having neglected
to extend you my thanks for your support during this
very trying period. Without question, you've shown
yourself to be that rarest of all creatures—a true
friend."

"Not at all," Reginald allowed, placated. "Happy
to be of assistance. The merest nothing."

Giles now seized the opportunity to insert neatly, "And I trust, then, that your interview with Miss Stebbing proved profitable?"

"Oh, quite," Reginald confirmed. "Simply not to be credited how easily we agreed on the best way for you to proceed," he said, plunging bravely into his role. "What I mean to say is, it appears Miss Lindsay would be more than willing to entertain your suit. Miss Stebbing is of the opinion that she has quite lost her head over you."

Giles appeared hard put to know how he should treat this announcement. He sat down with a jolt.

"Has she?" he managed after a moment.

"Well, practically bound to," Reginald continued airily. "Her only other offer was from her father's assistant, that rustic of a Pennington fellow. It seems the slyboots took advantage of her father's death to press for her hand. Not that one expects any different, of course, from an upstart." He sniffed disdainfully. "But to no avail, it turned out, because Miss Lindsay—quite properly, mind—refused to hear any of his tomfoolery. I wonder if that wasn't why she came to town in the first place. I understand she once called the man a puff toad."

"Did she?" Giles murmured, temporarily diverted. "And worse, too, I don't doubt, if I know that irascible tongue of hers. But however can I thank you? Why, dashed if I won't go at once and lay my case before her," he declared.

To Reginald's panicky dismay, he began to rise from his chair before halting at a sudden thought.

"Good God! I can't do that. She'll be expecting you, after all, not me."

Reginald began cautiously to relax.

Giles looked at him meditatively. "But it's only natural that she'd be awaiting her remuneration, don't you think? Mmm. Best have you pay the shot first," he said more cheerfully. "Besides, I daresay it might ruin my plan if I turn up like some spoony greenhead before the paint's even dried on the canvas."

"But Giles, I don't see—"

"What's more, I imagine Miss Lindsay would be pleased to boast a little soft of her own. Having a bit of the blunt might make it easier for her to receive an offer from a veritable Croesus like me," Giles concluded with a flash of inspiration.

"You may have the right of it," Reginald allowed. He tried to ignore the prickings of his conscience at having failed so far to mention the impending arrival of Horace Pennington. "I'll call on the lady tomorrow," he offered generously instead. "After all, shouldn't like her to think me a pebble peeler for not discharging my end of the bargain. What's more, be surprised if she don't prove uncommonly anxious to see you—that is, me."

ATHENA HAD PASSED a decidedly restless night, and the prospect of the new existence that stretched mercilessly before her had so daunted her spirits that it was close to noon before she made an appearance outside her bedchamber. She had even welcomed the task of arranging for her aunt the day's flowers in the dining room. With her bowls and vases and a heap of roses, she settled there gloomily, oblivious of their sweet scent and the glory of their intense yellows and pinks, pure whites and passionate reds. While her hands were busy with the flowers, her mind flitted here and there among her preoccupations.

She wondered how she would ever manage without the loving and sustaining atmosphere she'd discovered within the walls of Elizabeth's sitting room. She had managed to go on well enough before, she reasoned with herself, so doubtless she would contrive comfortably yet again. Even to her ears that belief sounded as fragile as the blush roses in her bowl.

But then she could scarcely claim that since arriving in Grosvenor Square she had managed her life very adeptly. Hadn't she barely extricated herself from one scrape only to land immediately in another? And wasn't it also true that she couldn't keep her mind off the man who had pushed her into those same scrapes? By her reckoning, the painting must have been in Giles Wescott's hands for nearly twenty-four hours, and yet he hadn't seen fit to communicate with her in any way whatsoever.

Really, she thought, snipping off a stem with unnecessary force, as if it weren't enough that he'd concocted such a ridiculous scheme in the first place, now he was making her wait for a response—as if her painting were of no more importance than say a shirt from a haberdasher's. And even though he might be reluctant to reveal the whole part he'd played, at least she'd expected he'd volunteer some comment on her work.

Why, she realized with a start, she'd never actually considered that he might not discuss her painting with her. Indeed, she admitted reluctantly, she was by this time thoroughly confused as to whether it was more hurtful for him to have repudiated her as a woman or as an artist.

It was perhaps for want of the means to resolve this question that her mind now swung from a disparagement of one man to a diatribe against the whole of his sex.

SUCH WAS THE UNPROPITIOUS atmosphere into which Reginald trod a short time later when he entered Lady Hollinwood's sitting room, armed with a neck-or-nothing air to confront an immovable Miss Lindsay.

"I expect," Athena said abruptly, "that you've come in response to my note."

"Yes. Well, no—that is, not precisely. Called at Miss Stebbing's first to pick up the goods, you know."

"Indeed," Athena said. "How happy I am," she added deliberately, "that my handiwork is now in the possession of its new owner."

Reginald wondered if this last comment deserved closer scrutiny but hastily rejected the notion. "That's the dandy," he agreed. "What's more, come to settle my account."

Athena's response to the news that her patron was prepared to touch the pocket was somewhat less enthusiastic than he'd anticipated. "What? Not a word about the picture itself?" she objected. "I must tell you, sir, that even a few morsels of praise are far greater payment for any artist than a whole lapful of guineas—although I, for one, should be equally glad of both."

This request caught Reginald notably unprepared. He had scarcely given the painting a glance. Fortunately, it occurred to him that a vicarious assessment might suffice, and he accordingly offered, "Afraid such judgments are quite above my touch, you know. But I believe Giles did remark on how you'd been carried away."

"What?" Athena cried, narrowing her eyes in a way that he found most intimidating. "'Carried away'?" she repeated in a furious voice. "Do you mean to say he thought I'd made a mess of the painting?"

"Oh, dear," Reginald inserted nervously. "I suppose I mightn't have perfectly remembered his words. Did he say 'carried it off' instead, I wonder? Yes, that must be it," he nodded, "because he never said you'd botched the thing up. But then, no doubt he means to call on you himself in order to discuss the matter," he added in an attempt to turn the conversation into a more agreeable channel.

After a peep at the unreadable expression on Athena's face, he went on gamely: "Fancy we settled on seventy-five pounds. Then I imagine this draft against my bank should serve. Though I must say the amount is a mere song compared to the result," he concluded in a belated, if commendable, attempt to set matters to rights.

And having to his inexpressible relief thus executed his appointed task, Reginald hurriedly withdrew.

IT WAS QUITE BEYOND HOPE that such a caller would be so fortunate as to have his departure escape the notice of all other interested parties. Although he urged his horses to a spanking pace from a standing start, Reginald's unmistakable figure was duly noted by the sharp-eyed Lady Hollinwood, whose carriage had just then turned onto the square.

Indeed, Reginald's arrival on the scene provided her ladyship with a curious new piece for the puzzle of her niece's activities. That very morning, in fact, she'd become aware that Athena's behavior had suddenly diverged from the pattern that had previously been established. Until now she had been uncertain whether or not the alteration was a purely temporary one. However, given the nature of Mr. Thurston's relationship to Giles Wescott, his presence at her house seemed to raise several intriguing possibilities.

The most credible of these, her ladyship decided, was that he was serving as a messenger between the two lovers. Another and more disturbing thought— that Giles Wescott had spurned her niece and that Athena had summoned his friend to heal the breach— also occurred to her. But since she would be able to determine which of these circumstances was correct only by biding her time a while longer, she resolved to adopt that course—provided matters demanded no more than another twenty-four hours before she could set her own plans in motion.

CHAPTER NINE

ACCORDINGLY, LADY HOLLINWOOD awoke at an unusually early hour the next morning in an attempt to steal a march on her niece. But her efforts proved profitless, for time crept by with the plodding determination of a snail circling a rock without Athena so much as stirring outside her bedchamber. The longer her ladyship listened, the more irritated she became at the callous behavior of a certain individual until she felt compelled to counter the shabby treatment being accorded her niece.

These emotions finally were sufficient to push her from her bed, through the intricacies of dressing and down to her carriage, fully determined to drive the matter to the wall before the day grew much older.

It was to her credit that this resolution accompanied Lady Hollinwood on the better part of the drive to St. James's Square. Still, the nearer she approached the house, on which the owner was rumored to have spent a tenth of his fortune, the less convinced she became of the noble nature of her errand. To be honest, her ladyship was obliged secretly to number herself among those who stood rather in awe of the formidable Giles Wescott. She suspected that he'd scarcely look kindly on an old lady's attempt to meddle in his private affairs. Nor did she truly believe that threats of scandal and ruination would push him a jot closer to reassessing his position, since it wouldn't be the first time that gentleman had chosen to fly in the face of the polite world.

Take, for example, the matter of his house, her ladyship brooded as her barouche moved slowly down Bond Street. Two years ago he'd suddenly bought it and proceeded to furnish it with the spoils of his travels on the Continent, awakening the hope that the town's biggest catch was at last preparing to acquire a wife. But when the question had been put to him directly, Giles had merely laughed and said his parents wouldn't have enjoyed seeing their own house cluttered with his collections. His new address was far more convenient to the other pursuits offered by the clubs along St. James's Street. Still, several young hopefuls had gnashed their teeth at finding the opportunity to become mistress of that enviable household slipping yet again through their fingers.

So it was understandable that her ladyship should now feel just the smallest flush at being on the point of infiltrating the building where Giles Wescott was said to dwell in an unparalleled splendor that excluded members of the fair sex.

Giles's house didn't exactly meet Lady Hollinwood's expectations. Lavishness was entirely absent. As it was, she was only conscious of feeling less on edge as she was escorted through a series of beautifully proportioned and what she later described as meagerly furnished rooms.

The climate of the house seemed, nevertheless, to agree with its owner, for when her ladyship was shown into Giles's study, she discovered him in pleasant contemplation of a large canvas that was propped against one wall. She was not sufficiently discerning at this early hour to note the haggardness about her host's eyes, which spoke of a sleepless night, or his stiffly controlled bearing, which hinted at a dramatic upheaval in his sensibilities.

Giles promptly assumed that Lady Hollinwood had discovered Miss Lindsay's pursuit of her artistic ambitions and had come to charge him with collusion. Yet her actions seemed to belie the notion, for she had so far done little but pointedly eye a couple of decanters on a nearby Pembroke table.

Interpreting this sign, Giles offered, "I was just about to enjoy a glass of Madeira. Perhaps you'd care for some ratafia."

Lady Hollinwood snorted derisively. "Never touch that water gruel if I ain't obliged to. I warrant the Madeira will serve very nicely."

After fortifying herself with a generous mouthful of wine, she aimed a sharp look in her host's direction and observed bluntly, "I expect you're wondering why the devil I'm here—eh, Wescott?"

"Not at all," he replied blandly. "Even a rascal like me may, on occasion, be honored by the attentions of a woman of the world."

Lady Hollinwood gave a pleased cackle. "So long as you don't term me a woman of the town, I won't worry."

Giles allowed his gaze to dwell in admiration on her ladyship's elaborate costume in varying shades of purple, which gave her a marked resemblance to both an aging courtesan and a dying iris. "Oh, there wouldn't be the slightest danger of making that mistake," he assured her innocently.

"I shouldn't be the least surprised if your tongue don't dish you up yet, Wescott," her ladyship observed dryly. "But never mind that. I didn't come to brabble. Got something important to discuss."

"First, perhaps, you'd be so kind as to tell me what you think of my latest acquisition." Giles motioned toward the canvas he had been contemplating, which showed a young girl nursing a baby and staring into the window of a carriage in which a lady was seated.

"Why, I fancy I've seen that very chit!" Lady Hollinwood exclaimed at once in surprise. "Or one uncommonly like her. Well, one can hardly avoid it. I couldn't count the times I've been out in my carriage and no sooner will we stop than there'll be some bit of a face staring in the window at me. Scarcely more than babes themselves, but they've got brats of their own already. Got that same look as this one, too—not asking, really, just watching. Enough to land you in a heap, I can tell you."

Her ladyship stared at the painting over her glass for a long moment. Then, recalling herself to her surroundings with a start, she tittered nervously. "I can't

think what you're about, Wescott, letting me spout off
a lot of silly lip wisdom.''

"On the contrary, I found your response most illu-
minating. The artist's talent must be considerable indeed if through a simple rendering of a familiar scene
we're led to discover so much more. The title of the
painting is *Portrait of a Gentlewoman*, but whether it
refers to the lady on the street or to the one seated in
the carriage, the artist—who is herself a woman—has
cleverly left to her audience to decide. The work is
truly in the grand style.''

Lady Hollinwood, having waited impatiently for the
close of this speech, now appeared to reach an important decision. She planted herself in a chair and declared peremptorily, "High time we stopped playing
fast and loose, Wescott. I've come, as you very well
know, to discover what you mean to do about my
niece.''

"Why should you think I intend to do anything with
her at all?'' Giles said calmly, his pulse quickening
nonetheless.

Lady Hollinwood fixed him with a withering stare.
"I'd never have credited that you could act so meanly
if I hadn't heard it for myself. It's one thing to lead the
girl a dance, particularly when I suspect she hasn't
been unwilling. But then to tip her the double without
so much as a by-your-leave or a particle of remorse!
Well! That I should have lived to see a gentleman capable of such underhanded dealing!''

Giles sat down behind his writing table and fanned his hands inquiringly. "And what, if I may ask, is the dastardly crime of which I'm accused?"

"It won't advance your case in the least to play the innocent with me, my boy," Lady Hollinwood responded vigorously. "Not when there's a witness to my niece's daily secret excursions from the house. Only one reason I know for a chit to go to such lengths. Past doubting you've managed to compromise the silly goose's reputation, and I mean to see you put things to rights directly."

"I finally begin to understand," he murmured. "On the testimony of this unidentified individual, you believe me to have been the recipient of these visits—no doubt as a result of having offered Miss Lindsay a *carte blanche*. I'm sorry to have to disappoint you. It's quite true that I'm guilty of leading the lady astray. But I assure you it's only her integrity that has suffered—and perhaps her conscience, too—but not, I promise, her honor."

"But I thought—" her ladyship began. "Well, it's beyond question that she's been seen to decamp each morning for some mysterious destination." She gazed nervously around the study as if willing its elegant contours to match this description.

"That she has," Giles confirmed, "but for quite another purpose. Miss Lindsay wished to pursue the development of her artistic talents. Knowing your ladyship's sentiments on that subject, she thought it advisable to keep her activities secret. I confess I freely assisted her—though she wasn't at all happy at having to resort to such a deception. In point of fact, her excursions have had no more smoky a destination than Miss Stebbing's house, where every morning for several hours Miss Lindsay has been at liberty to paint.''

''To paint?'' Lady Hollinwood repeated dumbly.

''Yes. And with notable success, I may add, as your ladyship has so recently testified.'' Giles waved a hand in the direction of the canvas.

''Athena painted that?''

''Indubitably. Here, you'll note, is her signature, 'A. Lindsay.' ''

Lady Hollinwood stooped laboriously to the signature and returned nonplussed to her chair.

''And there have been so secret assignations between the two of you?'' she ventured hesitantly.

''With the exception of those relating to the particulars of the painting, no, I regret to say—as Miss Lindsay would doubtless have confirmed had she been asked, which I gather she was not. Indeed,'' Giles added severely, ''the fact that you even consider her capable of dealing so lightly with matters of virtue is, if I may say so, utterly inexcusable.''

''You may not say so—'' Lady Hollinwood began crossly.

''And what's more,'' he continued, leaning across the table and directing a stern look at her, ''the least you can do is to tender an apology if not to me then to Miss Lindsay herself. Though who's to say when such incidents occur whether the blame ought more properly to rest on those responsible for the transgressor?''

"On those—?" Lady Hollinwood sputtered. "I'll thank you, Wescott, to keep a civil tongue in your head. I am going," she announced in an icy voice. "I didn't come here to be insulted. And I must say— though I had thought differently—that I'm altogether thankful there's no attachment between you and my niece."

"Oh, but there is," he inserted. "At any rate, I find that my affections are quite firmly engaged."

Lady Hollinwood goggled unabashedly at her host. "They are? I must say you've a deuced queer way of going about it. Or was that the motive behind all this painting business? I wondered, you know, how a man of your sensibility had become involved in such a bacon-brained scheme in the first place."

"I did commission the painting, it's true, but through a representative. For though I'd like to believe that I'm still able to separate my interest in Miss Lindsay as an artist from my personal interest in her, I thought it best to keep my role in that enterprise a silent one."

"How commendable," her ladyship observed tartly. "And I take it you've decided to deal likewise with your feelings, then, for I'm quite convinced Athena hasn't a clue as to their existence. Else why should she, at this very moment perhaps, be entertaining another gentleman bent on securing her hand?"

"What—now?" Giles bellowed as if stung. "Who?"

"Mr. Horace Pennington," her ladyship supplied with a triumphant smile. "The same who was until recently my late brother's assistant and—I'm given to understand—a most estimable individual.''

"Ha! That whiffler!"

"That he may be, and a tuft hunter, too, I shouldn't wonder. But I wouldn't underestimate the fellow if I were in your boots, Wescott. Why, who knows but what his persistence may succeed in breaching the castle walls—particularly when the lady ain't aware there's another knight in the vicinity.''

ATHENA WATCHED Horace Pennington cross the sitting room floor with niminy-piminy steps. *I'm sure I could forgive him looking like the fool if only he wasn't so disposed to act like one, as well,* she thought. At this moment she could scarcely muster a grain of patience for a visit that had interrupted her conversation with her aunt.

Upon her return from St. James's Square, Lady Hollinwood had lost no time before waylaying her niece and imparting, with considerable pride, the outcome of her interview with Giles Wescott. The news that Giles so much admired her painting was sufficiently surprising to Athena, given Reginald's sinister report of his opinion. But surprise had been quickly surpassed by shock when she learned that Giles not only admired Athena the artist but also had confessed that his affections were firmly engaged by Athena the woman.

It was understandable, therefore, that her good manners had been severely tried when Mr. Pennington's arrival had dragged her away from her aunt's boudoir immediately after this second—and crucial—announcement. Nevertheless, she succeeded in greeting him with a fair degree of courtesy and in dutifully inquiring how he was enjoying his stay in London.

"Oh, it's a decided change from my humdrum existence," Mr. Pennington enthused. "Not that I mean to decry your generosity in allowing me to continue at your home whilst I pursue my portraiture! And particularly not when it looks to be prospering. Lord Buckeley was so taken with my likeness of his daughter that he has helped me to secure a number of other commissions, as well. He has also invited me to call on them while I'm in town. But naturally I couldn't think of doing so until I'd paid my respects to your family." He gave her a meaningful stare.

"I can't conceive why you couldn't," Athena murmured absently, her mind drifting back to her interrupted conversation.

Was she safe in believing that her aunt was telling her the truth? she wondered. Lady Hollinwood had a weakness for unsubtle maneuvers and had been trying to throw her into Giles's arms for weeks. And Giles himself had deceived her more than once and hadn't balked at ruining her reputation with West and the others. Could he have told her aunt some fabrication in order to embroil her in yet another disastrous scheme?

"My dear Miss Lindsay," Mr. Pennington pleaded to attract her attention. "How could I hope to restrain myself from immediately rushing to your side?"

He proceeded in one bold move to throw caution to the winds and himself—though a trifle more slowly—to his knees. "If only I could convey to you how often I've longed for your presence beside me these many weeks! You must know that my only intention in coming to London was to discover whether you hadn't yet tired of this silly experiment and to do my utmost to persuade you to return home with me!"

"Experiment!" Athena exclaimed. "Sir, I must advise you not to continue any further in this direction." She glared furiously down at the figure kneeling beside her chair. "I will in no way entertain your suit."

The timely entrance of Lady Hollinwood's butler forestalled any response from the worshiper at Athena's shrine.

"Mr. Giles Wescott, miss," Scorsby announced with relish.

A delicious thrill coursed through her body, and Athena marveled at the independent way the heart operated. In spite of all the many reasons she had to disbelieve everything Giles had told her aunt, a secret part of her buried deep within her breast was even now madly celebrating his praise of her painting and his confession that he had lost his heart to her.

Not the least irritating thing, she thought distractedly as she watched him negotiate the floor in a half-dozen strides, was his knack for selecting the most inconvenient time for conducting a private chat.

Almost as if he'd heard her utter those thoughts aloud, Giles stopped beside Athena's chair, the better, apparently, to examine Horace Pennington's prostrate form. Bending into a polite bow, he offered her such an amused smile that she was hard put to keep her own face expressionless.

"I trust," he said blandly after Athena had made the introductions, "that I haven't chosen an inconvenient time to call?"

"Not at all," she assured him firmly. "In any case, I believe Mr. Pennington was just on the point of withdrawing."

Even that unimaginative gentleman had no difficulty in identifying this remark as a dismissal. Nevertheless, he managed to regain his feet and to retire in good order by saying airily, "Oh, quite so. But I'll return tomorrow, if I may, so that we may conclude our discussion."

"As you wish," Athena said in a colorless voice, "though I believe there is nothing much left to discuss."

"One wonders if Mr. Pennington can recognize a setdown when he meets one," Giles observed pointedly, when they were alone.

"I assure you it's not in the least becoming of you to make sport of your betters," Athena said crossly, in no mind to be kept in suspense any longer.

"That poor lapdog?"

Athena regarded him with disapproval. "How very unkind of you, sir, particularly since it was you who once pointed out to me that first impressions are so often misleading. At least Mr. Pennington may be applauded for being forthright in his actions. No one would ever think to charge him with concealing his true motives.''

"I fancy I detect the fine hand of Lady Hollinwood hereabouts, do I not?'' Giles inquired, narrowing his eyes in a way that was decidedly at odds with the mildness of his tone.

"It's true that my aunt has seen fit to interest herself in my affairs—and perhaps even to a degree that I have sought to discourage,'' Athena conceded. "Nevertheless, it's entirely proper that she should do so, especially when the matter bears so directly on the reputation of one of her relatives.''

"Do you know, I believe her ladyship must be a good deal more romantically inclined than I'd heretofore imagined,'' Giles said in an attempt to alter the thrust of the conversation. He sauntered over to the empty fireplace and swung around on her suddenly. "Else why should she have conceived the notion that these daily absences of yours were in the nature of— assignations, I believe she termed them?''

Although Athena was by now aware of the means by which her aunt had arrived at that conclusion, she was not inclined to allow him to turn such information to his own account. So she immediately sought to dismiss the question with a careless "Oh, I'd advise you not to refine upon it overmuch, sir. My aunt, as you well know, is one of those individuals who can imagine no worse a misfortune than for a woman of my age to remain unmarried and who, in consequence, would be likely to beat up the quarters of any gentleman injudicious enough to show a partiality for my company. Though I'm sure I hadn't thought your regard for me went any deeper, say, than a blood's for the favorite that miscarries in the first chase of the season. But then, of course, why should I have had even a clue, when you succeeded so well in concealing beforehand what I collect I'm now expected to believe are emotions of the most intimate and lasting variety."

"I fear it's quite true that I was misguided in trying to hide my very real admiration for you," Giles admitted. "But you can't tax me for that blunder any more severely than I myself. I assure you I've thought and rethought what must have been my reasoning in electing to stay wide of the mark. But all I can discover is that at the first I was reluctant to acknowledge that my feelings for you were not exactly those of a patron for an artist but rather those of a flesh-and-blood man for an altogether desirable woman." Athena forced her hands, which had flown up on their own initiative, to float back again into her lap. "And then later I was given to understand that you harbored no such sentiments for me."

Athena sidestepped the question implicit in his last remark. "I should think myself misguided if I developed an attachment for someone who has conducted himself in such a disingenuous fashion as you. It may be too nice a distinction for some, perhaps, but I for one could never look kindly on a gentleman who wasn't unquestionably worthy of my trust—as I believe I've had occasion to point out to you in the past."

"Well, dash it all, how else do you propose I might have assisted you, then?" Giles protested. "I knew your abilities weren't of the ordinary sort the first time I clapped eyes on your sketches. I merely employed poor Reggie's services because—as you've just recalled—I'd every reason to believe you'd reject an offer of a commission directly from me." He pushed his hand through his hair in exasperation.

"Very nicely put, sir." Athena kept her eyes off the one dark lock that fell irresistibly over his forehead. "To be sure, I applaud your supposedly lofty purpose—who would not? I only regret that your conduct hasn't always been guided by such extreme concern for my success. Indeed, it is your valuable assistance that has set me up as a castaway before I've made even the slightest advance against the current."

Observing Giles's baffled expression, she elaborated. "When wondering what course I might take after finishing your commission, it occurred to me to apply to the three most notable bodies of study to learn if I might be accepted as a pupil." One part of her watched with satisfaction as Giles's face became a dusky red. "You may well imagine my mortification," she continued relentlessly, "when I discovered that to a man the principals weren't inclined to grant a dispensation to the young lady who was possibly Giles Wescott's protégé but at any rate certainly his latest paramour."

"You don't mean to say you called on Varley yourself?" Giles inquired faintly. "And Leslie, too? Even," he continued bravely, swallowing with some difficulty, "even left a card at West's?" He prodded the fire grate with his boot, dislodging Athena's careful arrangement of flowers. "It's too bad you received their slurs in person. Still, it was practically bound to happen, you know, because dashed if I see how those three can lay claim to more than half a brain among them." Unsuccessful in his attempt to coax a smile from her, he said in a more serious tone, "But you must know that such insinuations weren't directed at you in particular, since I suspect the same treatment would have been tendered to any lady making similar inquiries."

"Surely you don't expect me to believe that I'm the first of my sex to ask permission to sketch at someone's elbow?" Athena said skeptically.

"No, nor the last, either, I trust. Yet I imagine it wouldn't occur at all to most hopefuls even to make such a request. And the others would reject the notion as being as impractical as skinning a flint."

Noting that Athena's face had relaxed a little, Giles pressed on: "And as to your being my protégé, why you're certainly that already, if you wish to be."

At this careless invitation Athena stiffened again suspiciously. "But how can you think I feel confident in your opinion of my abilities, sir, since by your own admission you've lately entertained thoughts quite at variance with those ordinarily shared by a patron and an artist? And what's more, you've seen to it by your arrogant meddling that I can't expect an objective appraisal of my work from anyone in the whole of London."

"Now that's coming it a bit too strong," Giles argued in turn. "Why you must persist in thinking that there is one way, and one way only, to solve every problem quite surpasses my understanding. And if it was arrogant for me to have made an honest, if blundersome, attempt to promote your career, particularly once I came to suspect my own ability to remain detached, than I'm happy to claim that distinction. But then I suppose that what they say is true: A man in the throes of a lasting passion may be counted on for only one thing—to act like a fool! However, now I believe it's high time for me to leave. I've no desire to persist in arguing with you—or even to persist in pressing my suit for the moment, since you appear to find it so very distasteful."

He took a step or two toward the door and stopped short. "But I can't leave without telling you plainly what I came to say. You have won me heart and soul. I'm finding it a rather novel sensation, but I would very much like to become accustomed to it." He came quickly over to Athena and gazed down at her. "My own dearest, you must believe me when I tell you I love you beyond question—and beyond sense or even propriety or anything else you might care to mention. So please, dear heart," he asked, taking her hand and raising it to his lips, "would you do me the very great happiness of saying that you'll marry me?"

Athena felt her heart leap. She let herself savor the sweetness of the moment before slowly and reluctantly drawing her hand away. "It's quite true," she admitted with some hesitation, "that I find your wit and intellect to be unsurpassed and your company and conversation a good deal more attractive than any other gentleman's of my acquaintance. In fact, it was only when I thought you and not Mr. Thurston were secretly betrothed that I began to realize the full extent to which my affections had become engaged. Nevertheless," she continued in a more decisive voice, raising her head and meeting his eyes with an even gaze, "I fear I must decline your offer, sir. You must see that I can't afford to let marriage stand in the way of my pursuing a serious career as an artist." As Giles opened his mouth to speak, she said firmly, "I don't wish to argue the point at the moment. I collect you were proposing to retire...."

"Oh, to be sure," Giles said in an equally determined voice, "though merely from the room, you know—not from the lists."

He executed a graceful bow and then withdrew.

Athena was left in a veritable puddle of confusion. Giles had nearly made her cast aside her normal caution, but she had managed to cling to her composure and gain time to think. Now that she was at liberty to weigh his apparent sincerity against her ingrained mistrust of him, though, her head was in a whirl, and she was only too relieved to be interrupted by the arrival of Elizabeth Stebbing and Miss Palmer.

"Oh, I've never been so glad of company as I am of yours today!" she cried as she came forward to dispense a kiss each to her visitors.

"Are we your first callers, then, love?" Elizabeth inquired slowly, made wary by Athena's brittle gaiety and by the spots of crimson that burned feverishly on her cheeks.

"No!" Athena exclaimed, waving them to seats and perching on the edge of a sofa. "Giles Wescott has only just gone. Oh, I almost forgot. My first visitor was Mr. Pennington."

"I imagine, from what you've told us before, that I can guess the purpose of Mr. Pennington's visit. But I own I haven't the vaguest notion what Mr. Wescott's errand may have been." Elizabeth regarded her friend closely. "Something to do with your painting, I expect?"

"In a manner of speaking," Athena said. "You see, my aunt apparently mistook my daily excursions to paint at your house for secret, romantic trysts with Giles Wescott. When she took it upon herself to visit Mr. Wescott in the hope of forcing him to agree to salvage my reputation, she also happened to let slip that a rival for my hand had appeared on the scene. And no sooner had I refused Mr. Pennington's unwelcome proposal of marriage than Mr. Wescott arrived to offer a rather more attractive one of his own instead."

She looked from one to the other, a rueful half smile playing around her mouth. "I can see by your faces that you're wondering why I'm not simply happy that the man who has captured my heart has said he loves me—loves me beyond sense, he said—and has asked me to become his wife—am I right?"

Her friends nodded silently in unison.

Athena jumped up and came to stand in front of them. "Don't you see," she begged, "how difficult it is for me to believe that he's altogether sincere? You both know how many times he has taken me in. He says he loves me—but he's said so many things that turned out to be false. Besides," she rushed on, sensing that Elizabeth was about to plead Giles's cause, "I haven't any notion of what he may think marriage ought to be. Why, he might expect me to put aside my painting entirely in order to manage his households. Or he might expect to oversee my career, so that I'd soon find myself obliged to paint only for those people he selected and only what subjects they wished."

She stopped abruptly, having frightened herself only too thoroughly. This gave Elizabeth a chance to say soothingly, "It seems to me, love, that you're confusing a particular question with a general one, the first being whether you wish to marry Mr. Wescott and the second being whether you wish to be married at all. Do you agree?" It was Athena's turn to nod in silence. "Now, you've said often enough that a woman's interests and endeavors outside the circle of her family are often curtailed once and for all by her marriage."

"Yes," Athena allowed, immediately changing sides and adding, "but his interests are virtually the same as my own, so what matter if he does ask me to put them first?"

"Precisely," Elizabeth agreed at once. "So you see that you have already answered the particular question, and the real issue is whether you wish to marry at all. And it seems to me the only way to answer that question," Elizabeth said bluntly, "is to consider what other choices may be open to a single woman, without money of her own, wishing to pursue a career."

Athena threw herself down on the sofa and buried her head in her hands. "It's enough to make me wish I'd been born without any talent or ambition," she said at last in a muffled voice, "and certainly without having been stupid enough to think that coming to London would solve all my problems!"

Elizabeth and Miss Palmer exchanged a glance of comprehension. Miss Palmer added a decisive nod, so Elizabeth inquired in a sympathetic tone, "And what, my dear Athena, do you mean to do now, if I may ask?"

Athena sat up and replied in an exhausted voice, "Oh, you may ask, but I'm altogether unable to supply an answer. I don't know what to do. I can't stay here. Mr. Wescott has already told me that he intends to persist, and I won't feel comfortable until I'm out of his reach and had a little time to consider what accepting his proposal would truly signify."

They all fell silent, Athena lost in thought and Elizabeth and Miss Palmer waiting fascinated and hardly breathing to hear what she next would say.

At first, Athena's mouth drooped disconsolately. Then she pursed her lips—considering what? Then came a very small smile, which broadened into a delighted grin.

"Elizabeth, my love," Athena said, her eyes beginning to sparkle, "would you consider, do you think, bearing me company on an unexpected journey? You see, I believe I've suddenly found myself obliged to pay a visit to the Continent!"

CHAPTER TEN

ATHENA'S VISITORS greeted this announcement with a mixture of awe and shrewdness in direct proportion to their respective characters. The normally reticent Elizabeth gave a little shriek of excitement. Miss Palmer, for her part, shot a piercing look at Athena before inquiring directly, "Not running away, are you, child?"

"Surely there's nothing wrong in wishing for some time in which to think things over undisturbed," Athena protested. "Besides," she continued more strongly as her plan took shape in her mind, "what better method to weigh my feelings about the matters we've just discussed than to provide a fresh setting and context untainted by previous associations? As we visit the sights, I can explore whether my view of married life could ever match that of my suitor. When we listen to music, I shall sound his words for proof of his veracity. And while we admire the paintings, I will sketch out for myself the possibilities of a career as an artist. Indeed," she concluded enthusiastically, "we ought to think ourselves fortunate that Mr. Wescott's proposal has provided the impetus for advancing one of our own instead!"

She smiled triumphantly. "Now, then," she continued in a more practical vein, "it shouldn't be difficult for us to obtain the letters of introduction that I understand are necessary for a sojourn abroad. Certainly among us, for example, we may know some individuals who've taken the grand tour or served in the conflict on the Peninsula."

This ill-timed remark dispelled a good deal of Elizabeth's enthusiasm. "However could I have forgotten?" She turned a disappointed face toward Athena. "We might as well leave off right now making any further arrangements, since I daresay Papa will never allow me to participate in such a scheme."

"But perhaps we won't have as much trouble as you think in convincing him of the wisdom of our plan," Athena answered, still elated. "Now I come to think of it, my aunt will most likely persuade him."

"I'm sure I don't see what profit Lady Hollinwood should find—" Elizabeth began.

"But then you don't have as nice an appreciation as I of her ladyship's priorities," Athena pointed out. "I wouldn't be at all surprised if my aunt were to wash her hands of me when she learns that I've rejected an offer of marriage from Giles Wescott. What better way than to send me off to the Continent? What's more," she continued optimistically, "since she can't let me go alone, she's very likely to wheedle consent out of your father."

ATHENA PROVED to be entirely correct. Indeed, Lady Hollinwood offered only the most token resistance before yielding gracefully to the plan suggested. In fact, she seemed so little disturbed at the announcement that the three ladies wished to travel together for a period on the Continent—save for directing a hard, measuring look at her niece—that Athena wondered if her aunt had already found out all that had passed in her house that day. Scarcely had the door of the sitting room closed behind her two guests, in fact, when Lady Hollinwood turned on Athena and exclaimed dryly, without any preamble, "I assure you—despite what you may believe—that I'm not yet a complete simpleton. I understand from Scorsby that Wescott paid you a call today—with what intent even such a poor dunderhead as you seem to think me may very well imagine. As if I couldn't guess what lies behind your sudden desire to sample the foreign scene."

Lady Hollinwood surged out of her couch and stared into Athena's face from a few inches away. "I take it the man made you an offer and you, for some inexplicable reason, refused him? Yes—I see by your expression I'm slam up to the mark. Well, I haven't a clue as to why you should have done so. The fact is, I don't think you even know yourself. And in my opinion you'd make a big mistake to think you'd be likely to encounter such a man as Giles Wescott again. But since you're clearly resolved to throw him over, that's all beside the bridge now—no need to discuss it further. You say you wish to quit London? Very well, you shall have your wish. And what's more, I promise I won't even attempt to counsel otherwise, since you obviously know best. You'll find me willing to do whatever's required to send you off at breakneck pace the minute you decide you're ready to go.''

Lady Hollinwood drew herself stiffly upright and pressed her lips firmly together to signify that she had finished.

Athena saw no reason to doubt that her aunt would do other than keep precisely to her word. Moreover, she knew the dexterity with which Lady Hollinwood maneuvered when she chose to apply herself to a problem. Otherwise, she concluded the following afternoon, she might easily have mistaken the speed with which that lady accomplished the necessary preparations for approval of her niece instead.

The day began with the arrival of Major Stebbing. On encountering him when he emerged from her aunt's apartments, Athena was surprised to find him in distinctly fine fettle. He didn't seem to be treating the dissolution of his household and the departure of his only daughter with either the gravity or the deliberation that those events surely deserved.

Not that she was meeting with much greater success in predicting the emotional state of any of the other parties involved. Even Major Stebbing's example didn't adequately prepare her for the appearance of his daughter, who pranced into Athena's apartment in the afternoon as boldly as a knight off on crusade. Since such an attitude was in marked contrast to Elizabeth's customary demeanor, Athena tactfully inquired whether her friend was feeling quite up to par.

On the contrary, Elizabeth assured her, she was in transports. After her father's conference with Lady Hollinwood, it appeared, he'd informed her not only that he would permit her to go abroad but also that he intended to escort the party himself. What's more, he'd already sent word of their imminent arrival to several of his acquaintances in Paris. He'd even, she confessed, flushing slightly, directed a letter to Squire Holt in Gloucestershire, asking him to keep an eye on their country house in his absence.

Athena noted the flush but tactfully refrained from commenting on it. Instead, she steered the conversation toward the more practical concerns of the moment. And since Mr. Pennington didn't make good his promise of a return visit, discussion for the next hour centered on such vital questions as how many cloaks would be required and whether each lady could pack all her belongings into a single trunk.

HAVING DISPATCHED all his letters, Major Stebbing, anxious to make known the forthcoming change in his circumstances, lost no time in setting out for Tattersall's. As it happened, Giles Wescott, also a habitual visitor to that sporting establishment, was there that day, too. Observing the major's exceptionally self-important air and eager to learn at once what was in the offing, Giles made a point of drifting over to where he stood.

After spending a few minutes exchanging companionable assessments of the various horses being offered for sale, Giles ventured, "Do I take it from your demeanor, sir, that you're thinking about embarking on some new enterprise?''

"Not thinking," Major Stebbing corrected. "Going. Abroad, that is."

"I see. Returning to the scenes of your successes, I shouldn't wonder."

"Wish I were," Major Stebbing said sincerely. "The thing of it is, my girl's suddenly become fixed on visiting the Continent, and I'm to escort her. Only proper, you know. Wouldn't do to have the ladies trotting about on their own."

"The ladies?" Giles prompted with increased interest.

"Never known my Beth to so much as venture across town without dragging her governess along, too. What's more, it appears the two of them have persuaded Lady Hollinwood's niece to join up, as well. Actually, Louisa's the one who persuaded me to let 'em go. But the funny thing is," the major said confidentially, "she told me she don't at all want them to go and she don't even think her niece much wants to go, either. But you know how it is—the more you try to force a horse to jump, the more stubbornly the fool thing will refuse. So Louisa's cramming the girl at the fence in the hope that the filly will back off of her own accord."

Giles shook his head in admiration for this magnificent image.

"Dead set against it myself at the start, mind you," the major continued. "It ain't ladylike, for one thing. And then damned if I know why anybody'd choose to go wandering about foreign cities if they ain't obliged to. Battlefields—well, that's another matter.''

"Indeed," Giles murmured sympathetically, intensely intrigued by this news. "But I can't say I agree with you, sir. I'm frequently subject to the urge to take myself off to some strange city or other. Of course, that's not the same thing as being obliged to haul three troublesome females around. Now, when was it you said you're to depart—?''

"Well, and that's the other hitch," Major Stebbing exclaimed irritably. "Only just been informed they mean to go, and then they tell me they wish to leave at once—tomorrow, or the day after. Why, it's plain as a pikestaff none of 'em has the least sense of all that needs doing before they set out. Got to order the traveling coach cleaned and rigged, got to bespeak a fresh pair at every posting house, got to—"

"To be sure," Giles interrupted smoothly. "But then I'm confident that a man as experienced as yourself will contrive to arrange everything perfectly, as always."

"No doubt," Major Stebbing agreed. "Best see to it, then," he said. "Though I've as much hope those three will be ready to leave at the appointed hour as I do that a piebald won't be distanced before the last pole!''

IN THE FOLLOWING two days, as he had promised, Major Stebbing set himself to deal with all the tasks that had to be completed before the travelers could depart—after his own fashion. But the major, having had a good deal more practice in planning military campaigns than pleasure journeys, had concluded that one trip was much like another and made his arrangements accordingly.

So it came as something of a shock when Elizabeth found that he had neglected to arrange for any overnight accommodations along the route in the expectation that the party was to travel around the clock like troops on a forced march. That oversight and others of a similar nature required immediate attention, and these errands had naturally devolved on the ever-practical Miss Palmer, since Elizabeth, though enthusiastic, was scarcely experienced in such matters, and Lady Hollinwood, though also willing, had ample work already to occupy her time.

Athena, curiously enough, was neither particularly busy with her own preparations nor especially enchanted any longer with the prospect of traveling to the Continent. She wasn't even wholly aware of the efforts being made on her behalf.

She had originally conceived of the idea for the trip quite spontaneously as a means of gaining time. Somehow, however, the more energetically Lady Hollinwood promoted the plan, the more Athena, without realizing the exact point at which her own enthusiasm had begun to fade, nearly lost all interest in it.

This morning, after getting up at five, she'd spent two hours with her head in her wardrobe, halfheartedly debating between packing two pairs of leather boots or one pair of satin slippers into her valise—her mind all the while drifting from thoughts of Giles and herself to thoughts of her future with as much direction as a leaf floating down a swollen stream. And then, as she had knelt beside her painting box, the brushes and crayons strewn around her on the floor, Athena's attention had wandered from her present predicament to her possible response and circled back again.

She had committed herself to going abroad and evading Giles, but now she longed to talk to him. What a fool she had been. How else could she discover if she wanted to marry him? And who else could help her learn to become a real artist and not just an amateur dabbler?

As she absentmindedly inspected her dirty hands and soiled gown, she admitted to herself that if she'd been daunted at first by Giles's resistance to all attempts by her to damp his ardor, she now found she was decidedly disheartened by the new evidence that he appeared to have thrown up the struggle entirely. He hadn't come near her for three whole days. And the resulting prospect—that she might have to leave London without being able either to answer his question or her own with any certainty—was, she had to confess, depressing indeed.

Athena was listlessly pouring water into the basin on her washstand, thinking that she might as well clean her hands since her packing seemed to have come to a halt, when Alice ran noisily into the room.

"A gentleman to see you, miss," Alice announced breathlessly. She shot her mistress a curious look. "Said he thought you might be expecting him."

Water slopped all over the washstand. Athena hastily laid down the jug and darted out. She flew down the stairs but stopped in the hall to take a deep breath and speak to herself sternly. So by the time she swept into the sunlit sitting room, there was no question of her flinging herself into Giles's arms or capitulating at the mere sight of him.

"Good morning, sir," she said calmly. "I fear you've discovered me quite disheveled. I've been trying to squeeze a second pair of half boots into my valise. No doubt as an experienced traveler you have learned to pack for a journey quickly, but I must say I find it beastly and fatiguing in the extreme. But then," she added politely, taking a seat on the sofa and motioning her guest to a chair, "perhaps you've not yet heard that I'm preparing to depart for the Continent?"

"So I've been given to understand. Indeed, that rumor was what prevailed on me in the end to pay you a call so very early in the morning," Giles explained in what Athena felt to be a rather ungallant fashion. He paused at this point as if he were in no particular hurry.

Giles had allowed himself to make the visit only after resolving to adhere strictly to his intention of offering whatever assistance he could to the travelers and keeping well clear of all other topics. But Athena's delightfully tumbled appearance and the shadows under her eyes made him waver.

Pretending to sample the contents of his snuffbox, he chided her, "Though I'd like very much to believe that you might have wished to tell me that news yourself."

"I can't think why I should have done so," Athena parried. "I believe our dealings with each other are at an end."

Giles pocketed the snuffbox, not surprised that Athena was still resisting hard. He had met many women more beautiful than she but never one the equal of her in spirit.

"But there you're surely mistaken," he said firmly, "particularly when we both know how rare it is to discover someone who shares a true affinity for the creative arts. Just as you have made a friend of Miss Stebbing, I intend to make every effort to nurture our friendship."

"Very well, then," Athena replied promptly, seizing the opportunity to get an answer to at least some of her questions. "Let us talk frankly about art and about our friendship, as you call it. Doesn't it seem to you that a woman is inevitably required to put the wishes of her husband and . . . and children before her own?" Giles nodded warily. "So tell me what reasons I might have suddenly to be willing to give up my artistic endeavors in favor of married life? Just how," she asked bluntly, "is it that you picture our marriage would be?"

"Here you are again with your either this or that," Giles objected. "There isn't any reason I can see why you shouldn't enjoy both art and ardor, shall we say, simultaneously. In the first place," he said, now as willing as Athena to fight out the argument, "I'm well aware that you'd little relish being wooed and won by a man who'd require you to set aside your painting as if it were merely a passing fancy or a simple hobby. In the second place, my own attempt at an artistic career taught me that those who are fortunate enough to possess a talent would never choose to forgo developing it. And in the third place, since art is one of the foremost things we share, how could you think that I'd expect you to do what I myself cannot do and give it up entirely?

"How do I picture our marriage? I picture marriage as a sort of partnership in which both parties agree to love and support each other equally in whatever each of them wishes to do, unconstrained by what custom dictates."

He laughed a little at her solemn face. "You needn't look so worried. There are such things as housekeepers and governesses, you know. You can dispose of your time entirely as you wish. Indeed, I'm surprised that you thought I could be so mean as to allow my sentiments in any way to impede your art."

"Well, to be honest, I never wholly imagined you to be a villain of such a deep dye," Athena allowed. "Still, it's not uncommon for a man to say one thing when he's courting and act another way entirely after he's wed."

"No," Giles agreed. "But despite what you may think of my performance in the past, I'm not commonly given to telling lies, you know. Perhaps you'd believe me if I were to offer to write the entire agreement down..."

Athena broke into a smile. "You needn't go that far. I think I do believe you."

Giles looked deeply into the pair of emerald eyes that now searched his face and decided to take a risk. "And is there anything else you believe?" he prodded gently.

"Yes. I believe...I believe that I love you, sir."

In a second Giles was beside her on the sofa. Possessing himself of her hands, he planted a tender kiss on each dusty palm. "And you will marry me? When? Next week wouldn't be soon enough for me."

"When. That's a harder thing to answer," Athena said, closing her hands on his. "You see, if I marry you now, I'll be an amateur painter for the rest of my life. I have only your opinion on my abilities. I'll never know if I have any real talent."

"And why do you think that?"

"Because," Athena replied, turning his hands over and working his fingers back and forth, "I'll never be able to learn to draw from a model and follow a proper course of study in a studio. My way to do so in London is barred. You know that as well as I." She gave him a ghost of a smile. "I'd have to study on the Continent and make a long, settled stay there."

"Yes," Giles had to agree. "You're quite right."

Athena was disconcerted. She tried to draw her hands away, but Giles held them tightly.

"Of course, there are still several drawbacks to overcome," she pointed out hopefully. *Not the least of which,* she added silently, *is the dismal prospect of being separated from the man with whom I've only just admitted wishing to share my life.*

"The cost of such a lengthy stay would be far beyond what I could hope to support. And it's impossible to believe I'd be allowed to live alone and to travel by myself."

"That is so." Giles thought a minute. "Which puts me to wondering whether you might be willing to entertain a suggestion of my own devising. Since I've already had the pleasure of supporting your first steps, wouldn't it be suitable for me to become your patron officially? As your patron, I could bear all the costs of your journey with whomever you wished to accompany you and also provide you with letters of introduction. My name is not precisely unknown abroad."

"Oh," Athena exclaimed uncertainly. "But that's most obliging of you, sir."

Yes, isn't it? Giles thought to himself.

"For example," he continued, "I've heard that Monsieur David is sometimes inclined to accept female students. I had the pleasure of making the fellow's acquaintance a few years back. So since you mean to pursue your studies abroad, perhaps a note directed to him wouldn't be amiss—if you intend to get as far as Brussels, that is."

At that query, Athena, on whom the mention of the famous painter's name had acted like a powerful drug, nodded dumbly. To study with David! She was dazzled by the prospect Giles was holding out to her.

"Oh, yes," she whispered, "that would be prodigiously great!"

"You may be perfectly assured that I mean to place no heavy strings on my help," Giles promised earnestly, unknowingly pressing her hands more tightly as he spoke and pressing beyond the limits of his credibility, as well.

No sooner had this remark been uttered than Athena abruptly regained her composure. Uneasily disengaging herself from his clasp, she observed in a voice that grew stronger as she spoke, "But why should you so selflessly place my professional ambitions before your own desires? How can you expect me to believe you? And if you honestly wish to marry me, why do you now appear bent on keeping us apart for years? There's something amiss with these offers of yours."

For once in his life, Giles was at a standstill. Athena's "I think I do believe you" and "I believe that I love you" were too uncertain, qualified, cautious, for him, and her reluctance to name a date was far from his own desire. On the spur of the moment he had determined to sweep away the last of her reservations and confirm his own belief in her talent with a bold, generous gesture—and his ingenious scheme had blown up in his face instead.

Once Athena had needed time. Now it was Giles's turn. Athena gave him a challenging look, and he decided to admit temporary defeat.

He bowed over her hand with undiminished aplomb. "I propose that we postpone this discussion until tomorrow—by which time I hope to present you with the means of confirming your true artistic worth and also my good faith."

Athena sat where Giles had left her, going over and over her dilemma until she could hardly think. She declined all her mother's efforts to coax her out into the sunshine to eat a little luncheon. But her aunt's butler was a privileged personage.

Scorsby threw open the door, and with what for him was an unusual display of feeling, announced with pleasure, "Mr. Leslie, Mr. West and Mr. Varley to see you, miss."

CHAPTER ELEVEN

WAS THERE EVER, Athena thought, a woman more burdened by circumstances over which she has had less control?

"I collect," she inquired bluntly as the three men filed into the sitting room, her patience having long since deserted her, "that there's some way in which I may be of service to you, gentlemen?"

"Oh, no," Mr. Varley replied effusively. "You might rather say we're all of us prepared to do a service for you, Miss Lindsay."

"But how very curious," she said with deliberate emphasis. "Each of you has already indicated that there's no way whatsoever in which I might avail myself of your services."

"But that, you see," Mr. Leslie put in, "was before—"

"Before we saw your painting," Mr. West interrupted, his rise from Pennsylvania born to London bred having made him a rather commanding figure. *"Portrait of a Gentlewoman.* Surely Wescott told you he planned to invite us to inspect his latest acquisitions from the Continent? He didn't? But I'd have thought— Well, no matter. We've only just come from his house. Once we'd been so fortunate as to discover the painting, we were in complete accord about not wasting any time before seeking an audience with its creator. And so here we are."

Concealing with some difficulty the shock that this speech afforded her, Athena inquired dryly, "I take it, then, that the picture met with your approval?"

"Brilliant!" Mr. Varley declared happily.

"Masterly!" Mr. Leslie exclaimed raptly.

"Quite creditable," Mr. West allowed, a shade less enthusiastically. "Though of course we weren't aware at the first, mind you, that the painter was a woman. Dear me, no—Wescott managed to conceal that little fact very cleverly indeed." He indulged in a reminiscent chuckle. "He slipped the canvas in among some others, you see, and never wagged his tongue even once as to its origins—not till we already had our necks on the block. We all of us thought it was the product of some poor wretch passing his days in reduced circumstances abroad. I mean to say, you can easily understand why we should."

"Oh, easily," Athena murmured.

"Naturally," Mr. Varley continued, taking up the thread of the narrative, "we perceived at once that it was a most superior effort."

"Naturally," Athena echoed.

"Precisely the sort of thing, for example, that we are used to expect from our members," Mr. Leslie inserted smoothly. "Which brings me to the other topic I was hoping to discuss with you. The Sketching Society is to hold a small and purely social evening on Wednesday next, at which time the members will display their most recent works. I venture to think—no, rather say I'm certain—that on such an occasion your painting should prove an instant success."

"Should it?" Athena said thoughtfully.

"All well and good, my dear Miss Lindsay," Mr. Varley advised with a disparaging sniff, "if you can be satisfied by scoring a hit among a row of ciphers of no influence at all. The Water-Color Society holds frequent exhibitions of our members' works by which means we hope to sway the opinion held by certain misguided individuals that water coloring is an inferior species of the art." He broke off to direct a cold look at Mr. West, who studiously avoided that gaze with the ease of much practice.

"Now to be sure," Mr. Varley continued, "I haven't yet been allowed the pleasure of viewing your watercolors. Nevertheless, I feel certain that any works of yours would be thought the centerpiece at our next exhibition."

"Do you truly?" Athena said curiously, wondering what the speaker would make of her studies of Kentish cows.

"Why, anyone but a perfect noddypoll could see that Miss Lindsay's abilities are of an infinitely higher kind," Mr. West noted impatiently. "In point of fact, the question is whether or not you mean to consider yourself a serious artist," he informed her, puffed up with his own importance. "As indeed are those painters who enjoy the sponsorship of the Royal Academy, since I trust even our severest critics will admit the influence of our exhibitions to be quite without parallel."

"Indeed," Mr. Leslie put in before Athena could respond. "And most uncomfortable they are, too. One is in constant dread of being nearly crushed to death by the visitors, most of whom have come to show off the clothes they are wearing rather than to admire the paintings displayed on the walls."

"Pray don't set too much store by the opinions of those who are sadly inexperienced in such areas," Mr. West advised grandly. "Certainly there can be no disputing the fact that a fair number of masterpieces have been found at our exhibitions."

"Oh, indubitably," Mr. Varley agreed. "Though I, for one, can scarcely begin to credit how. The paintings are mounted four and five high so that the uppermost row nearly reaches the ceiling, making the viewing of those pieces impracticable to all but a virtual contortionist."

Observing that Mr. West was readying a scathing reply and concluding that this exchange was part of a long-standing and obviously heated controversy, Athena hurriedly intervened. Promising to give their offers her undivided attention, she handed them over to Scorsby, still quarreling, and escaped to her bedroom.

There the accumulated strains of the day finally made her lose her temper, which she restored by throwing everything out of her half-packed trunk with satisfying crashes and thumps. She wasn't so green as to believe that her three visitors would have called on her if Giles Wescott hadn't made it plain that he was prepared to sponsor her, and nothing they'd said indicated that they truly believed her to be an artist of genuine talent.

However, Athena realized with a start, their invitations had suddenly rendered the possibility of achieving a successful career in London a good deal more certain.

Here, perhaps, was a solution to some of her problems, and a tempting one, at that.

Athena promptly determined to see whether Elizabeth had had any change of heart about leaving her home for foreign parts.

HAVING OCCUPIED HERSELF by enumerating the many benefits she felt might follow from remaining in London, Athena suffered a decided shock on reaching her friend's house. Elizabeth, it appeared, had just succeeded in banishing from her own mind a secret reservation she'd had against removing to the Continent.

The reason had more than a little to do with the unexpected arrival from Gloucestershire of David Holt.

He and Elizabeth had easily managed to overcome the difficulties posed by time and circumstance, and they were now seated very comfortably together on the sofa, Elizabeth curled happily into the curve of Mr. Holt's arm.

Athena's arrival didn't disturb their reunion in the least. Mr. Holt looked up quite readily at her entrance to smile at her in an altogether friendly fashion. And Elizabeth, after a vague "Oh, hello, love—was I expecting you?" was equally willing for Athena to sit down and join their conversation.

"No, indeed," Athena assured her in the too-hearty tone of one who wonders if her presence might not be superfluous. "I merely came to see how you were faring with your preparations," she invented.

"Oh, I fancy everything must have been attended to by now. Particularly since David's arrival," Elizabeth said cheerfully.

"I take it then, sir, that you've come with the purpose of helping us go off."

Mr. Holt shook his head. "No, I came to solicit Major Stebbing for Lizzy's hand. I've been fond of her ever since we were in the nursery, you see, so I could hardly be expected to watch her travel even farther away without making a push to settle things between us. Directly upon hearing the news of your departure, I came to lay my case before her father."

"And what do you think, love?" Elizabeth put in contentedly. "Papa has actually given his consent!"

"He was dead set against it at the start, you understand," Mr. Holt explained calmly. "And it's quite proper that he should want the best for his daughter, after all. The thing is, I was able to convince him that such was my wish, too."

Though she'd long ago suspected that Mr. Holt would snatch Elizabeth back to Gloucestershire eventually, Athena hadn't anticipated such a development at this time.

"I hope I may be the first to wish you both happy, then," she said, shaking his hand and stooping to kiss Elizabeth. "And do I apprehend, Elizabeth dear, that you're no longer interested in pursuing our plans?"

"On the contrary, love," Elizabeth assured her, "David and I have discussed matters thoroughly, and he's urged me to continue just as we've arranged. In fact, he proposes to become a member of our little party himself. He realizes that it's not likely we'll be afforded such a rare opportunity again. What's more, when he raised the idea with my father, Papa was overjoyed. David can escort us to the museums and concerts and all the other places Papa would most dislike, leaving him free to visit his friends and to wander around the battlefields to his heart's content instead. And when we return, David and I will be married and settle down in Gloucestershire to the peaceful existence we both so dearly desire."

"Yes, I see," Athena said faintly. She was guilty of a rather uncharitable wish that David Holt and Major Stebbing hadn't proved to be quite so accommodating. "It will be delightful to have your escort, Mr. Holt. But I had better return to my preparations, or you'll leave without me."

The implication of this last remark, however, wasn't completely lost on Elizabeth. "Didn't it seem to you," she asked Mr. Holt thoughtfully when Athena had gone, "that Athena might've had something in particular to discuss when she arrived? Maybe she has come to doubt the wisdom of going abroad or to resolve her feelings for Mr. Wescott. You'll recall, love, that I said I was sure she would do so eventually."

"But I trust that Miss Lindsay won't look to you to resolve that problem for her," Mr. Holt said, settling her more conveniently against his shoulder. "I'm not greatly experienced in such things, you know, but it appears to me the best solution would surely be the one she arrives at for herself."

As promised, Giles strolled into Lady Hollinwood's sitting room the next day with his customary poise, but as soon as he caught sight of Athena's pale face, he crossed the floor in a few hungry strides and bent over her tenderly. "But surely you've been unwell, my love."

Matching poise with poise and improving on Giles's performance, Athena fiercely resisted the weakness that overcame her at the nearness of his dark head and said coolly, "How very ill-bred of you to call attention to an imperfection in a lady's appearance, sir. It's only the everlasting preparations for our journey that have knocked me up so badly. As you know, I find myself far handier with a brush than with anything else. In fact, there seems to be some little call for its productions—or so I've recently been told."

"Have you?" Giles straightened with what Athena felt to be a maddenly self-possessed air and took up his favorite stance at the fireplace.

"You know perfectly well that I have," Athena said crossly. "I collect it was at your instigation that I was so unexpectedly honored by a visit yesterday from Mr. Varley, Mr. Leslie and Mr. West."

"It's true that I did undertake to discover if I couldn't pique their curiosity about the new painter in their midst," he confessed. "Still, if they hadn't been smitten with your talent and decided of their own accord to seek an interview, the matter would have ended then and there, for in that development, I'd no hand at all. But come now," he coaxed. "I'm half mad to learn the details of that fateful meeting. Tell me—were they not most complimentary?''

''Oh, decidedly,'' Athena confirmed grudgingly. ''Although my artistic abilities didn't, you understand, consume the better part of the conversation. No, indeed, that was given over to the most ridiculously childish brangling I've heard in the last twelve-month.''

''Proper bantams, aren't they?'' Giles observed. ''I don't suppose any of the three spared a word as to your future.''

''Yes, in a manner of speaking,'' Athena admitted. ''I may now boast no less than three invitations to submit my works to their exhibitions.'' She hesitated briefly. ''What's more, I confess I'm tempted to take at least one of them up on his offer.''

''What?'' Giles pushed himself away from the mantel and came hastily over to her. ''You don't mean to say that you're actually considering laying aside your plan to study abroad in favor of such a course?''

''And is there any reason why I shouldn't?'' Athena asked stubbornly.

''Oh, dozens,'' he assured her. ''But one of them is the most important, and of that you are aware already. Not one of your recent visitors will allow a woman to undertake their regular course of instruction, and if you won't be permitted to study, how then will you achieve an emotionless appraisal of your work and improve it?''

''But surely,'' Athena asked in a more subdued voice, ''I'd find some advantage in exhibiting my paintings?''

"Oh, without question," Giles agreed. "Though you would have to consider if the advantage was more than fleeting. I daresay you could sell a good number of your pictures. But I fear picture sales depend on whether or not you are in the mode rather than whether you possess talent of an extraordinary caliber. The same damnable thing applies to male painters, as well, you understand," he explained in an apologetic way. "However, when a woman painter falls out of fashion, there are fewer choices left to her than to a man."

"Yes," Athena said slowly, "it's all of a piece with the notion that members of my sex aren't yet to be considered true artists. Though I wonder, for that matter, whether I shouldn't find much the same attitude to be true on the Continent, as well."

"Perhaps to some degree—" Giles broke off and thrust his hand into his coat pocket. "I'd clean forgotten the reason for my visit. I've brought with me the letters of introduction that I promised you. One to David, four for Paris." He drew some closely written papers from his pocket and held them out to her. "Here they are. Do what you wish with them."

Athena reached out blindly for the letters and weighed them in her hand. "To M. David" was written on the top one in a bold scrawl.

She tipped her head back so that she could look Giles in the face. "Indeed, I find it hard to credit that you don't have some ulterior motive hidden behind your helpful exterior, sir. If you in fact love me, why do you wish me to go away?"

"Nothing could induce me to place a higher value on my happiness than on yours. So I'm ready to offer you whatever you might need to help you reach your heart's desire. You want to study on the Continent. There is your passport," Giles said, flicking his letters with one finger. "If you love me and want to stay with me…Athena, tell me without mincing words that you do."

"I do love you, Giles," Athena answered willingly, "and if only I could stay with you—"

"Why not try both, you silly goose?" Giles cupped her chin in his hand. "What's to keep me in England if you aren't here? Do you really think that I would stand on the shore and wave my handkerchief after you as you sail away? Unlike Major Stebbing, I enjoy foreign capitals, and I expect I can find enough to do while you're hard at work."

Athena broke into a radiant smile and, springing to her feet, clasped his hands in hers.

Giles brushed his lips across the hands resting peacably in his before at last gratifying his desire and gathering Athena into his arms for a deep, satisfying kiss.

After a long time had elapsed, he held her away from him and asked, "Is there any reason you can think of, my very dear Athena, why we shouldn't marry straightaway and travel together to the Continent for a leisurely honeymoon that will allow us to combine my collecting with your studies in an altogether agreeable fashion?"

"No," Athena said with perfect honesty, "I can't think of any objection whatsoever."

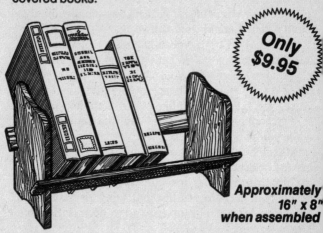

Take 4 novels and a surprise gift FREE

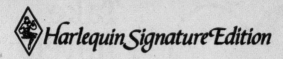

Violet Winspear

THE HONEYMOON

Blackmailed into marriage, a reluctant bride discovers intoxicating passion and heartbreaking doubt.

Is it Jorja or her resemblance to her sister that stirs Renzo Talmonte's desire?

A turbulent love story unfolds in the glorious tradition of Violet Winspear, *la grande dame* of romance fiction.

HON-A-1R